Dear Gav,

Things have been pretty busy here. Auntie Marg has taken so many photos already that she's going to have a few days off. Nothing to worry about. She's fine. Well, she will be. Hopefully. There was a teeny little crash involving Auntie Marg and a tuk-tuk (which is a sort of taxi), but don't tell Mam I said that.
The most important thing is that it wasn't my fault.
At all. Don't tell Mam I said that either.

Actually, DELETE THIS EMAIL, GAV.

Amy
x

www.randomhousechildrens.co.uk

Helen Skelton grew up on a dairy farm in the Lake District, and joined the *Blue Peter* team in 2008. Helen kayaked 2018 miles of the Amazon in 2010 for Sport Relief, and walked a tightrope between the towers of Battersea Power Station in 2011 for Comic Relief. She was only the second woman ever to complete the Namibian Ultra-Marathon, and was the first person to reach the South Pole by bicycle. Helen lives in Cheshire, and *Amy Wild: Amazon Summer* is her first book.

AMY WILD
AMAZON SUMMER

HELEN SKELTON

CORGI BOOKS

AMY WILD: AMAZON SUMMER
A CORGI BOOK 978 0 552 56839 5

Published in Great Britain by Corgi Books,
an imprint of Random House Children's Publishers UK
A Penguin Random House Company

This edition published 2015

1 3 5 7 9 10 8 6 4 2

Text copyright © Helen Skelton, 2015

Penguin Random House is committed to a sustainable future for our business, our readers
andour planet. This book is made from Forest Stewardship Council® certified paper.

Set in 12.5/19 pt Baskerville by Falcon Oast Graphic Art Ltd.

Corgi Books are published by Random House Children's Publishers UK,
61–63 Uxbridge Road, London W5 5SA

www.**randomhousechildrens**.co.uk
www.**totallyrandombooks**.co.uk
www.**randomhouse**.co.uk

Addresses for companies within The Random House Group Limited
can be found at: www.randomhouse.co.uk/offices.htm

THE RANDOM HOUSE GROUP Limited Reg. No. 954009

A CIP catalogue record for this book is available from the British Library.

Printed and bound in Great Britain by CPI Group (UK) Ltd, Croydon CR0 4YY

This book is dedicated to families.
The ones we're born into,
and the ones we build around us.

CHAPTER 1

I still can't believe he told on me.

Seriously, my brother is such a loser. Gavin's older than me, only by a year and eighteen days, but he goes running to Mam like a big crybaby when anything doesn't go his way. It's embarrassing! I mean, I know he had to give her an explanation – his eye was pretty much hanging out of his head. But he didn't have to tell her it was me who hit him. He *definitely* didn't have to tell her about the horseshoe I'd put inside the boxing glove.

I might tell his friends what a baby he is the next time they come over, just to see the look on his face. Billy and Jack are always at our house – we have huge football goals at the bottom of the farmyard, and Dad made us this brilliant tyre swing that two people can sit on at the same time. It was meant for all of us – Kate, Rebecca, Harpreet and me – but Gavin seems to think it's only for his farty friends. They're *gross*. They pick their noses when they're on that swing, and I know they do it in front of me so I won't want to go on it after them. It's horrid, but I'm not letting them bully me off it. I don't play on the rope swing at school because of that cow Sally Anne, so I'm not being bullied off a swing at my own house. (I would never call her a cow to her face, but she won't read this so I can say it here. I bet she can't even read). Anyway, with bogeys, as long as you wait until they're dry, you can just flick them off. Everyone knows that.

My friends don't come over much any more, to be honest. Their mams don't let them. According to Rebecca's mam, I am 'a disruptive influence'. I heard my mam tell her I was just 'spirited'. Go, Mam! I was proud of her for that – she never normally sticks up for me.

Gavin's friends still come over all the time. Which is unfair, because the things I get in trouble for are almost always *their* fault. Like, 'If you pinch those matches from your mam, we'll let you come camping with us.' I *always* get caught! Before too long I'll nail it, though – then they'll have to let me join in.

Just a few more weeks of school and then it's the summer holidays, and after that I'll be at the same secondary school as them. We'll all go on the bus together, Gav's friends will start to see that I'm OK – and hopefully my friends will be allowed to come round again. I really don't want to wear that stupid uniform, though. Sally Anne calls me frumpy already – when she sees me in that pleated skirt she'll have a field day. Still, who wants to look like a boring Barbie doll? All her friends have the same hair, wear the same lipstick and paint their eyebrows black. It's so boring. Last week I told Rebecca she looked stupid when she tried to wear her hair in the same sideways plait they all have, and she had a massive go at me. She kept saying I was jealous! I'm not – I could plait my hair and sit on it, if I wanted to. I never get it cut because it takes ages, unless Mam offers me a good bribe. (I'll go to the hairdresser's if she makes it worth my while).

It's days like that one that make me like hanging

out with the boys. Granted, they are TOTAL show-offs. Gav is the worst. He got picked to play cricket for his year, and he won't stop going on about it. It's like he plays for England or something. I'm only allowed to play now because I can overarm bowl – and that took me *ages* to learn. Gav used to tell me, 'You throw like a girl.' Idiot. I *am* a girl! And what does that even mean?! Anyway, I used to go down to the silage pit on our farm, where my dad stores the grass for the cows all winter, and practise until my arm was so sore I could hardly lift it. I never told Gavin, then I just went and joined in his game one day, and he couldn't stop me because they could all see I was pretty good by then!

Back to today. The thing is, Gavin and I fight. A lot. This time I am *really* mad. He grassed on me for going on the barn roof!

This might not seem like such a big deal, but I've been going up there for ever. I keep a stash of cherryade up there, and some sweets. It's the best hiding place on the whole farm, and the highest point – you can see everyone and everything from there: when Dad goes outside for a secret cigarette he thinks Mam doesn't know about; when Mam hides shopping in the garage she thinks Dad doesn't know about.

Gavin didn't know I could get up there until he spotted me this morning. He's such a chicken *he* wouldn't try and climb up – but if you scramble on top of the tractor when it's parked next to the barn, crawl along the first roof, climb through a gap in the tin and balance on one of the beams, it's easy.

Well, Gav's decided I shouldn't get to have a cool place because he doesn't, and he's told Mam, and he's *ruined* it. Jealous idiot.

I went mental, chasing him all over the farm. I knew that sooner or later he'd run round the corner of the garage – and when he did, I was waiting with my boxing glove. (We got them for Christmas from our Uncle Dave, who Mam says is 'Totally Irresponsible'. We have one each: Gav has the left one, I have the right.) I didn't even really have to take a swing, because he was running so fast that he smacked straight into the glove.

I didn't expect it to do so much damage.

It hurt me, too! I'd put a horseshoe in the glove to make it extra-hard, and it was rusty, so browny-orange bits flaked off and dug into my skin as Gavin's face bounced off the cracked red leather.

It's a shame, really. Without the marks on my hand I could have said it wasn't me. His word against mine, and all that.

'You've gone too far this time, Amy Elizabeth Wild. Too far! You could have taken his eye out. You could have blinded him!'

Classic overreaction. 'You could have taken his eye out'? How?! I don't have a pair of pliers and a spoon! She's such a drama queen, my mam – just like that flipping brother of mine, who is Mam's golden boy and favourite child. She drags me over to the bench in the kitchen that faces the door into the porch and makes me sit there while she tells me off. It's the door my dad will walk through after milking, and he'll meet my eyes, sigh and say, 'What now?' Sitting here, folded arms, anger bubbling up inside me, I listen to my soft-touch brother getting fussed over in the living room.

It's *always* my fault. I'm *always* the one who has to sit here, being told to *think* about what I have done.

I *am* thinking about it – I'm thinking how all I was doing was getting even, yet once again I'm the one in the wrong. Gav is *so* Mam's favourite.

It's OK – I think I'm Dad's, and I'm definitely Auntie Marg's. That's my dad's older sister. Although that doesn't really count for anything, because she has no real say; she's just our funny old hippy-ish aunt who lives at the bottom of the vegetable garden.

'I'm sick with worry all the time! Why can't you learn to behave yourself?' Mam witters on as she comes back into the kitchen.

'I was only on the roof looking for rare birds, and I was going to do sketches for my teacher!' I try to interrupt, but I stop when I see Mam's reaction. Hands on hips. Face clenched. She doesn't buy that for a second.

'Don't try and get out of this with a lie. You could have fallen. You could have broken your neck!' She actually looks quite upset now, and old. All of a sudden, my mam looks old. The lines around her eyes are dark and deep, her eyes glistening like she's about to cry.

'Oh, I get it!' I huff defensively. 'If I broke my legs you'd have to run around after me like you run around after Gavin, and you haven't got time for both of us. Only for him!'

Uh-oh. Too far.

I look from Mam to Bob, our shaggy Border collie. He can't even look at me, curled into a ball, his head resting on his front paws.

'To be fair, Mam,' I start to protest, 'the roof was actually quite a good hiding place, because—'

'*Don't get smart with me!*' Mam snaps. She's shaking with anger now, her face beetroot-red.

Mam is not normally as bad as this. Usually I get the Look – you know, when your mam says nothing but just stares at you in a way that makes your muscles freeze. You can't breathe because you know when you get home you are getting one hell of a telling off. Ever had that look? I hate it, but I'd prefer it to this rant.

Mam takes a deep breath. 'When your dad gets in we are going to have a serious talk about what to do with you. Now get out of my sight. I can't even look at you – you have really let yourself down today. You have let *us* down.'

Mam storms out, slamming the kitchen door. The plates in the dresser wobble and rattle. I think she might actually be crying.

She had to play the 'you let us down' card. That's the worst. When she yells, I don't mind. I feel bad when she cries. But 'you let us down' ouch. *Gavin* never lets them down; he makes them proud every single week. He's the best at everything: football, cricket, maths. Even flipping drawing.

I'd like to make Mam and Dad proud, but they just aren't proud of the things I can do. After all, that was an *excellent* hiding place. If we got invaded by an army, we could hide up there and I'd be the one to save my family and be a hero. For once. I'll point that out when Dad gets in.

Dad won't be *too* mad. He gets cross when I do something that makes extra work for him on the farm, like when I made a water slide on top of the black plastic sheet that protects the winter feed. That wasn't too bad, because I made myself cry when he was telling me off. He hates seeing me upset.

I can't turn the waterworks on with Mam, though.

She invented that trick. She knows *exactly* what I'm doing and it just makes her even madder.

For now, though, I can't just sit on this bench and wait for Dad to come in. I'm off to Auntie Marg's caravan. She'll know how to win Dad over; she always does.

CHAPTER 2

Auntie Marg has lived at the bottom of our vegetable garden for ever. She spends a lot of time in our house, but then again she grew up here, so it's kind of her house too.

She's meant to help Mam on the farm, in the house, with us. But she doesn't. She's left us at the school gates a few times, not because she forgets, but she just gets caught up taking her photos. She can spend hours watching a bird or a frog, and when she's close to the perfect photo she can't just abandon it, because the perfect photo is worth waiting for, apparently.

Her caravan is only about a hundred metres from our house. I can see it from my bedroom window. It's pretty ugly from the outside, with funny windows that don't open. Inside, though, it's amazing. It's packed to bursting with treasure from all over the world: a peacock feather from India; a tribal stick from Uganda; scarves and sarongs in every colour you can imagine.

She's not precious about it. I go in there and nose through it all the time, and she doesn't mind. 'That's from Bolivia,' she'll say casually. 'I found that in Bangladesh,' she'll add, as I pick up rocks and stones, holding them in the dappled light breaking through the tacky net curtains she refuses to replace.

It's a really old caravan now. Auntie Marg bought it when she was twenty with her first big pay cheque. She used to get paid to go all over the world taking photos for magazines and newspapers. She was a big deal back then. She hasn't been on a proper expedition for years, though; all the people she used to train up and take along as her assistants get the gigs now. 'I've had my day. They'd laugh at my efforts now!' I've heard her wail at Mam and Dad. One of her old assistants is the editor of a big magazine now, and he asked her to go and do some 'new stuff' recently, but she freaked when she got the email from him. I heard Mam and Dad saying she's lost her confidence. (I earwig a lot!)

I don't know why she doesn't go away on trips any more. I know she misses it. She looks at her photographs all the time. She's got boxes and albums and piles of prints, newspapers and magazines, all with *Margie Wild*, a place and date printed boldly on the back: *Margie Wild, Namibia, 1978. Margie Wild, Chile, 1969.*

She'd go off for weeks, sometimes months at a time. Once she lived with a load of women in an abandoned school in Tanzania. She went to Cuba to take pictures of some people she said we could all learn from, and once she followed families in Mongolia up hills on horseback.

It would be good if she went on the road again, so I could prove to my friends what a cool auntie she really is, rather than just some funny woman who floats about in long skirts, occasionally popping up at christenings and weddings. She hates all that family stuff, but Mam and Dad sort of make her go along. They think it will help get her back into it.

When I push open the door to her caravan, Auntie

Marg is sitting at her laptop, tapping away, a frown on her face. Her fingers are covered with silver rings, her long red hair knotted and messy. A bit like mine, except I'm blonde. 'Hello, my darling,' she says as I plop down next to her, but she seems distracted.

'What are you looking at?'

She sighs. 'The photographs from that Egypt trip that I didn't go on. It just looks so wonderful.'

'Again?' I say. 'Auntie Marg, you've been looking at them all week!'

Before Christmas, Auntie Marg had talked about going to Cairo. Some friend of a friend was filming pyramids for a TV company, and Auntie Marg was going to take photos for publicity or something like that. She loves creepy stuff – the idea of dead bodies wrapped in bandages that have been sealed in a tomb for thousands of years really excites her (although can you imagine how much they must stink?). It was the kind of photography she'd love to be doing again. But the friend of the friend asked someone else as well, and they said yes immediately, *and* got the money for the plane ticket together more quickly, so Auntie Marg missed out. Whoever that person was must have been pretty good because the photos have been everywhere, in loads of different papers, and the first time Auntie Marg saw them she burst into tears.

The caravan door swings open again and Gav sticks his head inside, grinning. Unsurprisingly, he doesn't look to be in pain at all. 'How long are you grounded for, then?' he asks me, smirking.

I leap at him, jump on his back and grip his head tightly between my arms, then push my thumb into his bruised, swollen eye. 'You're fine! I knew you were fine!' I yell into his ear.

'ARGGHHHHH! Get off me – that kills!' he snaps, throwing me down to the floor, onto my back.

'What are you going to do, tell Mam again?' I shout.

'Darlings, my darlings!' Auntie Marg tries to shush us. 'Please, stop fighting. Your mother will hear you! Look – we'll put something on the telly and all watch it together. How does that sound? Look on the Sky Plus thingy, Amy – I might have recorded something good.'

Scowling at Gav, I pick up the dusty remote control and switch the TV on, flicking through the channels.

Auntie Marg shouldn't really have so many channels in here but Dad got her an illegal aerial thing.
Mam doesn't know, and we aren't to tell her either.
Even Gav is in on this one as sometimes he sneaks in
here and watches football until midnight. On school
nights.

'Ooh, what's this?' says Auntie Marg as a creepy,
shadowy, steamy jungle fills the screen.

A man's deep voice booms. 'We are now deep
inside the Amazon.'

'Where you buy books?' I ask.

'The place, you idiot,' says Gavin, punching the
top of my arm so hard that even my fingers tingle.
'The Amazon rainforest.'

The voice continues. 'This creature kills with one
bite. You won't see it, but it will know exactly where
you are. It's a powerful beast that can swim, climb
and run, and ambushes its helpless prey. With one
snap of its jaw, the caiman can and will break your
hand.'

'What's a caymarrn?' I ask.

'Shhh!' Gav and Auntie Marg hiss in unison, both
staring at the telly. The picture has changed to a

murky-looking river surrounded by trees, a pair of piercing yellow eyes sticking out of the water.

'Oh, so it's like a crocodile?' I say. 'Cool!'

Gavin grabs the remote from me and starts to fast-forward, whizzing between shots of snakes and jaguars, monkeys and lizards. He zooms through a section all about huge, furry black spiders, not even stopping to listen to the voiceover. Gav HATES spiders. I'm not the least bit scared of them. I use this to my advantage as much as possible. If I can find even a harmless little daddy-longlegs in one of the barns, I keep it in a jam jar in my room until I hear him go to the bathroom in the night, then I sneak in and leave it on his pillow. He doesn't always see it, but when he does it's excellent!

I snatch the remote back from him and hit play.

The voice booms: 'At night the caiman, snakes and jaguars hunt for food, pouncing on unsuspecting creatures, tearing them from limb to limb. However, there are larger, more dangerous forces at work in the shadows. Forces that cannot be fully explained. It's said that many legends roam the riverbanks.'

'Oooh, this sounds fascinating,' says Auntie Marg, leaning forward.

An eerie, high-pitched wail echoes through the caravan. 'The legend of *el tunchi* is one of the most famous,' the voice continues. 'Hundreds of walkers have lost their way, following the shrieks and cries of what sound like people calling to them from the tree-tops. Locals claim they are the spirits of those who took their last breath within the Amazon. Many don't make it out . . .'

'Don't make it out? Where do they go, Auntie Marg? Does he mean they die?' I ask. Both Gavin and I are now staring at the screen.

'Shhh, listen!' Auntie Marg replies excitedly, hovering above her seat.

'*El bufeo colorado*, the pink river dolphin of the Amazon, is real enough, but some say they are more sinister than they look. Are they really dolphins, or are they men trapped in the bodies of dolphins, destined to lure children to drown . . . ?'

'What?!' says Gavin.

'That's weird,' I add. A cool feeling creeps over my body. The two of us are sitting side by side, more calmly than we have in years, our breath deep, fear in our lungs.

We watch the second half of the documentary. Our bums are numb but we are unable to move, fascinated and freaked out in equal measure. As the booming voice details more myths and creatures, it has us all gripped. 'And finally, there's *la lupuna*,' it says softly. 'A tree that is sacred to the people living in the Amazon. Many communities are built around it, believing it has magical powers to protect them and their families. It will punish anyone who disrespects them. Poison them . . .' Scenes of a steamy jungle fill the screen. The fierce yellow bloodshot eyes hold our gaze again, and the voice echoes around the caravan: 'The jungle is dense and full. Animals remain undiscovered, plants untouched and stories unexplained.'

The picture freezes and a list of names roll up the screen. We are silent, stunned.

Auntie Marg jumps to her feet. 'This, my darlings,' she says, grabbing my shoulders with both hands, 'is going to get me back on the map! Didn't you hear what that man said? "Animals remain undiscovered, plants untouched and stories unexplained!" This is *it*! I need to go there. With my camera, I will capture it all, the beauty, the magic!'

'Auntie Marg, there are Google maps now – you can just put the postcode in and have a look that way,' I offer, but the sound of her silver bangles clanging together as she waves her arms drowns me out.

'I will never photograph another wedding again – I will be the photographer I once was! Now, I need to immerse myself in the culture. I need to learn as much as I can.' She skips towards her laptop, her fingers fumbling over the keyboard.

Gavin's back in control of the remote now, and is whizzing backwards and forwards through the programme to find the biggest bugs.

'So creepy. So intimidating. So *wild*. I love it!' says Auntie Marg, bashing at the keys.

'What are you looking for?' I ask. She's not completely rubbish at computers like Mam, but I know I'm better. I edge closer to her and lay one hand on the laptop. 'Give it here. I'm quicker. I'll help you,' I offer, snatching it from her grip.

'Look for those amazing snakes, and the adorable

little monkeys. Look for *el tunchi* – how spooky! And what was that other thing called – *la lupuna*, I think? Incredible – a tree that can poison you if you dis-respect the jungle! The pink dolphins, too! Did you hear that bit? People believe that the pink dolphins are really the trapped spirit of a man trying to steal children – or did he say children trying to steal . . . Anyway, let's Google it . . . and then I'll find out how much the flights cost!' With every word, Auntie Marg gets louder, her bangles clattering, her pitch so high I think only Bob will be able to hear her soon.

'I want to know if there are really fish that can swim up a person's stream of wee and get inside them and eat their insides!' shouts Gavin over the excite-ment. His back is to us, his eyes on the football match now filling the screen. 'Are there really vultures that can peck your eyes out and eat them for tea?' he continues.

Vultures . . . fish . . . poison . . . Amazon . . .

I'm typing as fast as I can.

CHAPTER 3

'Some of the spiders are so poisonous they can kill you just by crawling over your hand,' hisses Gav from just outside my bedroom door. 'You won't even know it's there. It will feel like something's tickling you, and then—'

'*Gavin!* Shut up! You're only jealous. Just because Auntie Marg chose *me* to go to the Amazon with her! I'm not even scared of spiders, I'm not a chicken. Get lost. I have to pack.'

Although I don't really know *what* to pack. It's not exactly Spain or Scotland, is it? We once went to Spain, but we can't really take long holidays because of the farm. I once got invited on holiday with Harpreet's family, but just before they booked it I set fire to our cat (*by accident!*). As punishment

Mam and Dad said I couldn't go.

This is different, though. Auntie Marg has said she *needs* me. She needs my help – and I *will* help. Gavin keeps saying I'm going to muck it up, but I won't. I will not break anything or smash anything. I'll be the one they're all proud of. Gav is going to be sick of hearing Mam say, 'Amy was so useful on the trip to South America. Marg couldn't have done it without her!'

Mam's not quite at that stage yet. Unsurprisingly, she's *really* nervous about me going to South America with Auntie Marg, and she was dead against it at first. Auntie Marg suggested it the night we watched that documentary. She popped over after tea, when Gav and I were getting ready for bed. Mam and Dad think I can't hear it when they 'discuss' things, but Gav and I worked out years ago that if you sit at the top of the stairs with your head through the banister railings, you can listen to whatever's going on in the kitchen.

'It might be a good way to channel her energy, Janet,' I heard Auntie Marg offer.

'Energy?!' screeched Mam. 'You try dealing with her energy for more than a day and you'll change your mind about wanting her to come! She gets into enough trouble in our back yard. God knows what she'll do on the other side of the world! This is a *ludicrous* idea.'

'Margaret, I think it's time you went back to your caravan,' Dad cut in. 'Let me and Janet discuss this alone.'

Auntie Marg left the kitchen, her bangles jangling so loudly I missed what he said at first. Then Dad said, 'Marg has a point,' and suddenly I was listening very carefully. This was getting interesting. 'Maybe it *would* be good for Amy to have a bit of a job, keep her busy,' he went on. 'Keep her out of trouble. Marg's right – she has a lot of energy to use up, and – well, she hasn't got too many friends at school at the moment. That Sally Anne has been causing her trouble, and her other pals aren't really allowed to come over because of Amy's behaviour, so she'll only end up here all summer by herself, pestering her brother and his friends – and we know how disruptive she can be when she's bored.'

I DON'T PESTER THEM! I wanted to scream down the stairs. They're a bunch of show-offs who need putting in their place! I only hang out with them because – well, I'm sure once I get to secondary school I'll have *loads* of people to hang out with. A frown is hurting my head.

'I thought if we sent her to drama class over the summer, she might make some friends, you know? Get a bit more sociable?' Mam said.

DRAMA CLASS! I screamed inside my head, biting my tongue to keep myself quiet. I can't think of anything worse. I went once: Rebecca and Harpreet made me. They spent an hour faffing with their hair and make-up beforehand, then everyone talked about how they felt, and then we spent the rest of the time impersonating trains and tractors. It was stupid. They don't actually *do* anything. What a waste of time!

'Think about it.' Dad's voice was softer now, so I could barely hear it. 'This could be good for both of them. Marg thinks she's helping Amy, but maybe Amy would be a bit of a security blanket for Marg? This is the first time we've seen Marg excited about a trip in years!'

'You can't be serious.' Mam spat her words at Dad. 'It's hundreds of miles away, and you know how accident-prone BOTH of them are.'

Dad's voice was firm and calm. 'This could be exactly what both of them need. Marg isn't as batty as she comes across, and she's very experienced; and Amy needs a bit of focus, something to keep her busy, otherwise she'll go off the rails. I caught her swiping matches from the kitchen the other day.' I couldn't see him, but I was sure he'd have one hand resting on each of Mam's arms as she folded them across her chest. He does that a lot.

'MAM! DAD! Amy is listening to everything you're saying!' Gav shouted, inches from my ear! He'd snuck up behind me, the little snake!

'Shut up!' I hissed. 'They haven't decided yet!' I threw my arms around his head, muffling his mouth and nose, and Gav kicked out at my legs as he tried to get free.

The kitchen door swung open, and Gav and I scrambled from our positions, wriggling backwards and trying to get out of Mam and Dad's sights.

'Can't you two just get along? EVER?!' Mam yelled, her words fraught and angry as Dad pounded his way up the stairs.

'There's no way you are spending six weeks in this

house together. You'll kill one another. Amy, you're going to go and *help* your Auntie Marg,' said Dad firmly, one hand on my arm and the other pressed against Gavin's chest, stopping him from launching himself at me. 'It's decided!'

'But that's not *fair!*' Gavin whined. 'Amy gets in trouble and she gets a *holiday.*'

Dad glared at him. 'It is *not* a holiday,' he said firmly. 'Amy will have to work very hard. As for *you*' – he narrowed his eyes – 'you're going to be busy this summer. Helping *me*, on the farm. The summer's a busy time, and I need you to help. Just like Auntie Marg needs Amy for *her* work.'

Dad couldn't see my face, so I stuck my tongue out at Gav. We both knew that my trip *was* going to be a holiday.

Of course it's going to be holiday! Isn't it?

Even packing for the trip a few weeks later, Auntie Marg is managing to create a massive mess. She stores her photography equipment and travelling stuff in a spare room in our house. She's pulling things from every drawer, shouting out the names of random items as if she expects them to fly out for her: 'Mosquito net!' 'Sunglasses!' 'Water purification tablets!' Nine times out of ten, super-organized Mam is standing behind her with the item she is looking for.

'Don't forget to take extra for Amy,' I can hear Mam chirping as she follows Auntie Marg around the house, second-guessing what she needs. 'Remind her to put sun cream on every day. She's had all the injections she needs, but you'll need to make sure she takes her malaria tablets . . .'

Auntie Marg has had injections for every kind of tropical disease known to man – she had one in her bum once! I had mine in my arm. It hurt way more than the nurse said it would. 'Just a tiny little scratch,' she promised me. Liar!

Rebecca, Kate and Harpreet are being weird about my trip. I don't know why I hang around with them sometimes – they'd never go on a trip like this. They keep talking about all the snakes and spiders and fish with teeth that can bite your finger off (they saw it on YouTube).

Harpreet's having a birthday party while I'm

away. Her mum is letting them camp in the garden, and some of the Year Sevens from our new school are going. Rebecca said they're going to get a massive speaker and attach it to her brother's iPhone. They're having a huge barbecue too. They're talking about it like it's the party of the year. Even Gavin said he's going to go! He said he heard that Sally Anne is going too. I don't see how – she isn't friends with any of my friends. I don't think.

'Your mates are going to find better friends, so by the time you come back you won't know anyone,' he told me, smirking all over his stupid face.

Idiot. My friends would never do that to me. Never. But I Skyped them the other night to show them the new kit Mam got me for going away and all they could do was show me their stupid countdown calendar to the party. *Boring.* I said I had to get back to my packing.

Mam went and bought me a backpack two weeks ago – it's a proper geeky one, with a waist strap and a waterproof cover. Right, I've got cherryade and chocolate biscuits. Spare hair bobbles. Everything I should need.

There's a snuffling sound in the hallway outside my room. 'Bob?' I call. 'Come here, boy.'

I can hear Bob's paws pad softly across the landing. His tail's high and wagging and his dark eyes are wide as he comes into my room. He's always glad to see me. 'Remember who your favourite is while I'm away. Here's a clue: it's *not* Gav,' I say, burying my face in his stinky, matted fur.

A blob of dog drool drops onto my hand. I'm going to miss Bob.

I am excited. Well, I'm telling everyone I am. It's a massive adventure, and surely Gav and his mates will be impressed if I see a spider or a snake? Even Rebecca and Harpreet, and maybe even Sally Anne will stop giving me such a hard time if I come back having seen a jaguar. That's cool, isn't it? I wonder if they'll be allowed back to my house if I can say I've seen a jaguar up close?

CHAPTER 4

'It's not that exit, Richard! The next one!'

Auntie Marg is practically screaming at Dad through the gap in the two front seats, her big bottom wedged in between me and Gav in the back.

Mam's getting more stressed too, leaning over the handbrake towards Dad. 'Do you think we'll make it, Richard? Will they miss their flight? They have to get a connection at New York and then Lima. If they miss this first bit of the journey, all the rest—'

'*Enough!*' Dad shouts. 'All of you!' His knuckles are gripping the steering wheel so tightly they're white. 'If you hadn't forgotten your passport, Marg, we would not be running late. Janet, I know they have a connection to make, but we can only go as fast as we can go.'

Auntie Marg flops back against the seat, pushing me and Gav up against the doors. It's a tight squeeze. In the past Dad always drove Auntie Marg to the airport when she was off on one of her trips, but today everyone's coming to wave us off, so we're all packed in our smelly old Land Rover. (It smells because even Bob came along for the ride. If I have to say goodbye to Gav, I'm *definitely* also saying goodbye to Bob.)

Gavin leans over and hisses, 'You know we're going to Nando's on the way back, after we've dropped you off. I'll probably get some new trainers before we go home too.'

'We're going to be so busy having adventures that we won't even have time to get in touch with you lot,' I snarl back, pushing the nerves to the bottom of my stomach, pretending I don't care, acting as though I'm not the least bit worried about going away with just Auntie Marg – but let's be honest, she can't even make a pizza without setting herself and the kitchen on fire, so I have my doubts about how she'll get on in an Amazonian jungle full of terrifying predators. In truth, I feel like I'm getting on a rollercoaster. I'm telling everyone I'm excited, but

I'm a bit scared. I can tell because I need a wee all the time. I get like that when I'm nervous. What did that voice on the telly say? Something like, 'Few can explain the legends that roam the riverbanks'? Is that a good or bad thing? I think it might be bad.

Auntie Marg is just staring ahead. I think she's nervous too. This is kind of a big deal. The people at the magazine that published the Cairo pictures that Auntie Marg missed out on have told her that if she gets something good from this trip, they might work with her again. They said if she could do a 'Myths and Legends' piece, they'd even think about a book deal to collate a lot of her work from over the years, but they needed something new before they could go ahead. Auntie Marg started out excited, but I think the pressure's got to her – she had a serious wobble a few nights ago.

'Marg. You have nothing to lose!' I heard my dad reassuring her in the kitchen when Gav and I were meant to be in bed. (I only got up because Bob peed on my bed and I had to hide the sheets before Mam saw, otherwise she wouldn't let Bob sleep in my room any more.)

33

'But what if I've lost it, Richard?' Auntie Marg sobbed. 'What if I'm no good any more?'

I crept along the hallway and peered around the kitchen door. Auntie Marg was clinging to a glass of red wine and Dad was gently trying to peel her ring-clad fingers off it.

'Marg, this could be a *real* opportunity for you. You'll love it when you actually get there!' Mam added.

I didn't hear the rest of the conversation, taking the opportunity to hide the dog-pee-stained sheets.

Today, now that the day is finally here, Auntie Marg is jittery with nerves, but also excitement. Like Mam says, this is such a good opportunity for her to get back into what she loves to do. When Mam whispers to Dad, 'Their return flights – did you check whether they can come home earlier, if they need to?' Auntie Marg interrupts, 'No, no, we'll need *every* second. We have to earn the people's trust. We want the *real* Amazon. We're not tourists. We need to get beneath the skin.'

'*Real?* I'm pretty sure it's all real. It's not like

Disneyland, Auntie Marg. There won't be any fake bits!' I say, laughing.

'We're going for something more intimate. More special,' she says, more to herself than me, her eyes glazing over. So this is Auntie Marg in work mode. I've never seen this before.

We make it to the airport just in time to make our first flight. Mam is insisting on a big public goodbye: hugs and kisses at the counter, where a robotic-seeming woman wearing way too much pink lipstick takes our bags and checks us onto the flight. Auntie Marg is the oldest person here with a backpack by far.

'OK, thanks for bringing us and all that,' I say, shoving my snivelling mother towards the exit. 'I love you, but you have to go *that* way, and we need to go *that* way, so . . .' I point out that we *need* to go in opposite directions if we are going to make this flight. I love my mam, I really do, but she stresses way too much, and the more she stresses, the more I'm starting to realize how much I'm going to miss her. All of them. I need them to leave, quickly, before I start to get upset. 'Look, Mam, those security guards have spotted Bob. I don't think he's allowed in here,' I add.

Here she comes for one last hug: 'Just be helpful, Amy. Auntie Marg needs you.' She's sniffling and snorting back tears in between words. 'Look, here's a portable battery charger for your phone, so you'll never run out of battery. I know you love taking photos on it, so now you'll be able to take lots, and remember to call us. And I got you this little pouch to put it in, and wear around your neck. You know you lose your phone a lot, and this is waterproof and shockproof and . . . well, Amy-proof. The man in the shop said it was very trendy.'

She hangs the world's ugliest phone case around my neck. I look like a total geek now. Backpack *and* phone pouch. Seriously, all I need's a cagoule and a bum bag.

'Mam, I don't think it's for me,' I begin. I'd never wear this normally – my friends would kill me – but then I see Dad urging me with his eyes to keep it. I know that face, those slightly widened eyes and subtle nod. *Humour your mother.* 'Thanks, Mam, it's perfect,' I say instead, biting the inside of my mouth to stop myself from saying a word that would get me grounded for a week.

Gav awkwardly thrusts a present at me too. 'Here.'

Mam must have made him give me it, but it's actually kind of cool. It's a little pack of colourful cards: they are Top Trumps for the Amazon – AMAZON MYTHS AND LEGENDS. I quickly flick through them. Each card shows a different animal or creature or thing that may or may not live in the Amazon; there are about thirty of them. The capybara, the jaguar, the scorpion – I know those creatures are real. But some of the mythical, more mysterious things on that programme we watched – the river dolphins, the tree that can poison you, and the trapped spirits in the jungle – well, they're in here too. They're good, these cards.

'Well done, Gav,' I say reluctantly.

'Yeah, well, it's something to keep you entertained when you're not busy *working*. Get used to hanging out with Auntie Marg – we're moving house while you're away,' he says before turning away, dragging Bob with him through the glass door.

'He doesn't mean it, Amy, ignore him. He's just jealous,' my dad says, kissing me on the head.

'Well, he should be jealous, because we're going to have an adventure and I'm going to see snakes and wrestle crocodiles and other cool stuff, so you can tell him that when you catch up with him and *my dog*,' I shout at Gavin's back.

Dad places a hand on my shoulder and I realize he's upset too. Why are they all so flipping upset? *They* are the ones who decided to send me on this trip! 'Look after your Auntie Marg. You're there to help her, remember? And she needs this to go well. You both do,' Dad finishes.

Another kiss on the head. Another tearful hug from Mam. It's just her tears rubbing off on me, I'm sure it is, but now my face is wet too, and I've got that tingling feeling at the back of my eyes and my throat is hoarse and tight. I grab my bag.

'Auntie Marg, let's go. Come on!' I say, grabbing one end of her floaty scarf, causing the rest of it to tighten around her neck. 'Sorry!'

Without looking back, I pace towards the queues, the sea of families with cases and passports, pushing over each other to get through security to their planes.

I need to be in the crowd, swallowed by its chaos, so that Mam and Dad can't see me any more, so I can't see them.

Otherwise I might just cry.

CHAPTER 5

'In the event of a loss of cabin pressure, place the mask over your face and nose and breathe normally . . .' says a posh voice over the tannoy.

The words fall on deaf ears as people throw bags into the overhead lockers, shuffle blankets, wrestle cushions and try to settle into their seats.

'Auntie Marg, have you ever been in a plane crash?' I ask. I didn't think I was speaking particularly loudly, but the man in front (who, by the way, is *definitely* wearing a wig) turns to glare at me.

'Amy! You can't say things like that here!' she tells me quietly but firmly, gritting her teeth.

'I know! I'll take our first photo,' I suggest, pulling my phone from its ugly airtight pouch and flicking it to the camera setting. 'Look, I can switch straight to sepia tone . . . or black-and-white. Loads of different colours!' I lean over to show her. 'Selfie?' I ask.

I can smell the 'medicinal' wine Auntie Marg glugged down in the airport lounge, before we even got on the plane. She'll order another once we take off and then she'll sleep. Hopefully. She's not acting like herself at all – it's like my scatty hippy aunt waved us goodbye at the airport along with Mam and Dad. This Auntie Marg is tense and wired, full of nervous energy, with an excited, determined gleam in her eyes that I've never seen before. This trip clearly means a lot to her.

'We'll get some great photos, and then we can show off to everyone, can't we, Auntie Marg!' I say, nudging her. 'Your old photography friends – the ones who you used to be able to boss around. Gavin. My teachers—'

'It's not about showing off,' Auntie Marg interrupts. 'It's about – well, it's about me feeling *useful* again. I've been at the bottom of that garden like a mushroom, getting bigger and older in the shade for years. I need to prove I can do something again. To your mam and dad. To myself.'

'That's the same as showing off, isn't it?' I reply, but she doesn't seem to hear me.

To be honest, I'm surprised she didn't make a comment about all the different camera settings on my phone – Gav and I get that *a lot* from Auntie Marg. 'That is such *lazy* photography, darling,' she tells us. 'And so quick. I've shown you how to really develop a photo, in my caravan. Remember? There's nothing like the anticipation, the excitement as the image takes hold of the paper you're printing it on, and you see what you've got.'

You've never seen anyone care as much about cameras as Auntie Marg. She carries around a heavy camera with a clunky lens for one photo, another lens for a different type of picture. In fact, she carries about four lenses at once, all of them wrapped in suede cloth, all better looked after than anything else she owns. She dusts them, cleans them, protects and preserves them, treating them like rare delicate fossils. She's a different person around her precious camera kit, and she's a different person now she's on this photography mission. Already she's got her head down, scribbling lists, sketches and ideas in a stocky spiral-bound notepad. Things she hopes to see: dolphins, piranhas, sloths, native tribes. The list is long! I spot *el tunchi* and *la lupuna* on there and get a funny shivery feeling. Does Auntie Marg really think we'll find those things?

'Cabin crew, seats for takeoff,' says another voice over the tannoy.

Auntie Marg tucks the notebook into the pocket of the seat in front and starts flicking through one of the thick, heavy books about the Amazon she's brought along.

'Why don't you just use my phone?' I offer, pulling up web pages on birds and bugs you're likely to see in the jungle.

Auntie Marg's squinting at her book. 'Now, what on earth does that word mean?' she mutters.

I peer over her shoulder and read the Spanish word she's pointing at.

'Hang on!' I say. I lean across her and place my phone over the page she's looking at. 'Watch this,' I tell her as I swipe the screen to open a new Spanish translation app I downloaded last night. She's got to love this.

The screen of my camera focuses on the word, there's a second's pause, and the English translation pops up. 'It says: *flesh-eating fish*. You don't even have to look it up in a proper dictionary, or even that phrase book Mam made me put in my bag! How cool is that? Hold. Hover. Read! See, I'm already being helpful.'

I can do that – be helpful, I mean. I can carry things for her, get her water, make sure her batteries are charged. I know I can. Maybe Mam is right – maybe my 'energy' is better spent helping my loony loveable auntie rediscover her inner genius.

'So what's the plan when we arrive? Straight to the beach?' I ask Auntie Marg, half joking, half serious. 'Do you think they have Nando's in Iquitos?' I add. Also half joking. Also half serious.

'We're going to meet our guide at Iquitos airport. His name is Dudu.'

I spit my free pretzels out of my mouth. 'Dudu?! What sort of name is Dudu?! Isn't that "poo" in baby speak?'

'*Amy.*' The unusual firmness is back in her voice. 'Stop that. Once we've met Dudu, we're going to stay one night in a hotel, and then we'll start exploring Iquitos the next day.' She gives a little shiver, a shrug of her shoulders that sends a ripple down her arms and causes her bangles to jingle.

Maybe it's the wine, but I think she's excited. Actually, now that the tearful goodbye in the airport is over, and we're strapped in and ready to take off – so am I.

Dear Gavin,

I've got a bit of signal on my phone, so I just thought I'd send you an email to say hello and that we got here safely and that I'm not missing you one bit.

We just got off our third plane in two days! After we left you, we got on a massive jumbo jet. I watched three films, really violent action ones that Mam would never let us watch at home. I had three packets of peanuts, two packets of pretzels, three Kit Kats and two cans of Coke, and when everyone was asleep I went and asked the cabin lady for an extra snack and she gave me two chocolate bars.

Then we landed in America. You've never been to America, have you?! That airport was SO busy. I even had to tie Auntie Marg's scarf to my bag, otherwise I would have lost her.

Then we got on a slightly smaller plane and went to South America, to a place called Lima. Where, according to Auntie Marg's book, people eat guinea pigs! (We didn't. I told Auntie Marg I would NEVER eat a guinea pig, even if my life depended on it. We had a McDonald's.)

Then we got on ANOTHER plane. We had to carry our own bags onto this one, though. There were only twelve seats and three windows, but I got to sit next to one.

We flew over the rainforest and It's amazing, so much bigger than on the telly. It's not as green, and the river is way muddier. It's really brown and really bendy and really wide. When we flew over it for the first time everyone went quiet. I haven't seen any snakes yet, but that would be stupid – we were miles in the sky.

The airport we landed at when we reached Iquitos is nuts. They just chuck your bag off the plane and you get it off the tarmac yourself and then you have loads of people offering to help. That's when we met our guide, Dudu. He's kind of square-looking. He drives fast. You would like him.

I can't wait to get into the jungle. It looks so massive. The river is massive and the trees are massive, so the snakes must be massive and the spiders, well, they must be gigantic!!! I bet there are spiders here as big as YOUR head. Just something for you to think about when you go to sleep tonight.

Love you not.
x

CHAPTER 6

'*Bienvenidos a Iquitos!* Welcome to Iquitos!' says the captain.

As Auntie Marg and I step off the plane a massive wall of hot air smacks us both in the face. Even my lungs burn as I breathe it in. I could eat five of those massive Mr Whippy ice creams, it's so hot. Actually, if there was an ice-cream van here, I'd get some Mister Freeze ice pops to put under my armpits and in my pants. I'd put another on the back of my neck – it's *that* hot.

I'm sweating so much my hair is soaked already. I don't smell, though – no, a quick sniff of my armpit and I definitely don't smell, but I'm still sweatier than ever before. Auntie Marg's fanning her face with her passport. Her red curly hair has exploded into a

huge ball of frizz. 'It looks like your head is on fire!'
I laugh.

'I thought I was used to this kind of heat!' she
answers breathlessly.

Iquitos airport is kind of weird. There's no fancy
airport building or guards checking passports. No
conveyor belt delivering our luggage. You climb out
of the aeroplane onto the runway, walk across the
blistering tarmac, and head to your bags. It's almost
as if the aeroplane has done a poo on the edge of the
runway – a big pile of bags and boxes dumped on the
edge of the tarmac. It's chaos! It's so, so different to
the airports in Manchester and America we've just
come through. They could all have been the same
place: shiny floors, white walls and floor-to-ceiling
glass.

Auntie Marg leads the pack of passengers looking
for their bags. Unlike her, most of them are young,
maybe nineteen or twenty. All of them are wearing
the kind of sandals and sock combination we won't let
Dad wear on holiday, and most of them are wearing
bum bags. At least I'm not wearing a bum bag – but I
do have this stupid plastic pouch around my neck.

'Tabitha, grab my rucksack, babes!' one of the tallest passengers shouts.

'Harrison, honey, take a photo!' a girl wearing a headscarf calls as she leans against the pile of bags and poses.

'*Get off!*' Auntie Marg bats the girl away crossly. 'That's expensive kit you're climbing on!'

'Hey, take a chill pill,' offers the bloke taking the offending photo. He's got blond dreadlocks halfway down his back. 'There's no need to stress out. There are bigger things to worry about in this world . . .' he goes on. I think I just threw up a bit in my mouth. *Take a chill pill!* Who actually says that? *As if!*

'Oh, just buzz off and have a wash!' Auntie Marg snaps – she didn't say 'buzz' but something much ruder – turning her back on the pair and diving straight into the piles of backpacks and boxes. The spider's web of tangled handles and straps makes it difficult for her to find and free our last bits of luggage.

'That wasn't like you, Auntie Marg!' I say, impressed by her efficient aggression. Normally she's the one who wants us to hug it out and think about 'the bigger picture'. Not today. Then there's that language! Who was that?! This version of Auntie Marg means business.

'There it is! That's the last one!' she pants, grabbing a black case. 'Eight, nine . . . and you've got the hand luggage? Right, let's go.' She rolls her eyes at the gang behind us, now posing and piggybacking each other as one of their friends snaps away on a camera with a massive twisty lens.

Approaching the front of the airport, I can see a man striding towards us with purpose in his pace. He's holding a piece of cardboard with MARGARET WILD written on it. So this is Dudu.

He's meant to know what he's doing, and he certainly looks like he does. He's wearing baggy shorts, a tiny vest that barely covers his nipples, and flip-flops. His massive calves stretch one in front of the other, tanned arms swinging like a soldier. His neck is as wide as his head. He's definitely *walking* like a soldier, kind of stiff and square and upright, like someone stuck a pole down the back of his trousers. Gav did that to me once – shoved a broom handle down my top and trouser leg. I fell over and couldn't get up, but that wasn't even the worst bit – it gave me a massive splinter in my bum that Mam had to get out with tweezers. (I kept the splinter and put it in Gav's cornflakes the next morning.)

Dudu nods to Auntie Marg and starts lifting our luggage onto the roof rack of a funny little vehicle next to him. Auntie Marg flaps and tries to help, but he waves her pale chubby arms away with a meaty hand. '*Relájes*, Margarita. *Permíteme!*' he says, taking the last bags from her and gesturing for her to get into the vehicle. Margarita? Did he just call Auntie Marg a cheese and tomato pizza?

'What *is* that?' I say to him, pointing at the vehicle. It's a bit like a small tin taxi, half-car, half-motorbike, with open sides and a grubby canopy stretched over the top. All around us, passengers from our flight are climbing into similar vehicles with Spanish-looking drivers.

'My tuk-tuk,' Dudu declares proudly, his lilty accent bringing a smile to our faces. 'Our vehicle for the next few days.'

'Can I drive!?' I ask.

'Darling, get in!' Auntie Marg tells me. 'We have work to do!'

We climb onto the crusty back seat. Auntie Marg has one massive camera bag on her lap, the strap around her neck, while Dudu has fixed the others to the top of the tuk-tuk. The steering wheel is large and solid, and there is a windscreen – but no window wipers. I realize there's no radio either, so I swipe the screen on the phone around my neck and play Little Mix through my earphones as loudly as I can.

Dudu jumps aboard and the tuk-tuk bounces under his weight. His tanned foot hits the pedal, and we burst forward. With the high-pitched squeal of the engine underneath us, the wind whipping through the tuk-tuk, me and Auntie Marg sit back against the scratchy cracked leather, my shorts riding up so my thighs rub on the seat.

I stick my hand out of the side, and the wind against my outstretched palm makes it impossible to make a fist. It might look like this little thing has been patched together from scrap metal by my grandad, but it can move!

We whizz along the busy dual carriageway, with

heavy log-laden lorries overtaking us on both sides. Our little vehicle swerves in their wake, we're totally exposed – but it's exciting. 'I could touch the back of that lorry, Auntie Marg!' I shout over the thunderous noise of the vehicles and the beat of the music coming from my phone.

'DON'T YOU DARE!' she shouts back – but she's smiling.

From the busy road, we roll onto a dirt track dotted with farm buildings. It's warm. It's loud. It's busy. It's all so different, but then I guess we are millions of miles from home. I pull up maps on my phone and click the 'find me!' option. The pin flies across the globe and lands on a chunk of land below the USA, a thick bright blue line running along the edge of the little screen in my hands. That must be the river. Funny – it didn't look blue from the plane. It looked murky and dark and deep.

'Look, Auntie Marg! We're . . . well, we're miles from home, aren't we? On the other side of the world!'

Auntie Marg is shaking her head at me. 'You're missing it!' she tells me, snatching my phone and tucking it back into the pouch around my neck, the ear buds yanked out of my ears. 'You'll miss everything if you keep looking at your phone!'

'Wait, I might need my translation app!' I argue, but her hands are too quick. Besides, she's right – this place is exciting and there's so much to see. Already.

We're approaching rows of houses: tall buildings with fancy windows and fancy people crossing the road in front of them. Everything is so bright, so colourful. The buildings. The people. The tuk-tuks. Ours is green, but we pass orange ones, red, blue. Each one is packed with people, most of them with thick dark hair and huge smiles. Some of them wave back at me, others just look confused.

Occasionally we slow down just enough to see the houses – well, the porches outside them, at least. Most of them are packed with people too – including babies and old people – as well as having lots of hammocks, the occasional cat, and plenty of dogs. All of the dogs have long, skinny bodies and short orangy hair. They're nothing like Bob.

These little tuk-tuk things make a constant

neoooooooow-type squeal. They never stop. Then there's the laughter, spilling out of big-bellied men sitting on the street, drinking from thick brown bottles. All of it's peppered with beeps and toots from cars and taxis. There's a lot of shouting – not angry shouting, whatever it is the men are saying is met with smiles from the glamorous ladies. The ladies here are like old movie queens, with bright red lips, big bouncy hair and high shiny heels. They saunter across the street as the tuk-tuks lurch and leap past. Rebecca would LOVE these women. I snap away on my phone, taking pictures to show her.

We're closing in on the hotel now, and what must be the centre of town; the rows of wooden houses have turned into taller, fancier-looking buildings. Dudu is waving and shouting, '*Hola!*' He seems to know everyone.

The hotel we're pulling up at has fancy patterns around the windows, and a shiny set of steps leads from the pavement to a pair of glass doors. It's nothing like the photos of the places Auntie Marg usually stays in. She's always telling us she likes to 'get under the skin of a place' as she hates tourists;

she calls hotels with wifi 'hell holes'. This place has *definitely* got wifi. Which is good, because maybe I can Skype home and my friends and tell them how awesome this place is going to be.

Although . . . maybe Gav and my friends won't think I'm quite so adventurous if I Skype them from here. No – I won't get in touch.

'Auntie Marg, why are we staying here?' I ask, leaning out of the tuk-tuk. The high-pitched squeal drops a bit, and the tuk-tuk stutters and stops. Dudu pulls our bags off the roof and dashes across the road, saying that he'll be back in a second.

Auntie Marg, wiping her beaded brow, replies, 'I couldn't find us rooms anywhere else at such short notice. Just one night here. I need to check all the camera batteries are charged, and I want time to talk to the people in Iquitos and see what they can tell us before we head to the river.'

I'd told Rebecca and Kate and Harpreet all about the Amazon river. I told them how I would get a picture with a caiman and how I'd probably get to drive my own boat, but they didn't seem that impressed. They just kept talking about piranhas! They read on the internet that when the river is low, the piranhas get really hungry.

From the aeroplane, the river looked so much bigger than I expected. The jungle, running along either side of it, looked bigger than it did on telly too. Bigger, darker and, to be honest, a bit scarier. There's a lot to think about. My Top Trumps cards prove that. Flicking through them at the airport was one thing, but being here, everything I've read about feels a lot more real. There's *el tunchi*, and that crazy tree, and the lost walkers, and well, it just seems a lot wilder than I thought it might.

'The river sounds cool and everything, but *this* place – Iquitos, I mean – looks awesome,' I try, gesturing to the colourful houses facing the hotel. 'We could spend a week here, easy. I bet there's loads to do. There's a postcard shop across the street, look. We could always just get some of those photos, and can't you use Photoshop to add me and the caiman?'

'What?' says Auntie Marg, frowning. 'Don't tell me you don't want to do this. All you've been saying since I persuaded your mam and dad to let you come along is that you can't wait to tackle the jungle. You knew that was on the schedule – a day here, and then onto the river and into the jungle. We've got days to explore it, and you've been bragging about it to your brother and your friends for weeks. What's changed?'

'*Nothing.* I'm not scared or anything,' I insist. 'It's just . . . well, my cards say that there are snakes in there that can eat you whole, and there are spirits that can confuse you, and force you to get lost in the jungle, and if *that* happens then we'll never get to take your photos back to show everyone. You'll never get published again. So really, I'm just thinking of you, Auntie Marg.' Obviously I won't let her see that I'm feeling nervous, but I'm willing her with every bone in my body to realize that we might have bitten off more than we can chew.

'Oh, Amy! Come on, where's your sense of adventure?' she tells me. What's happened to my dotty old aunt? Who *is* this woman?

Her reassurance is interrupted by Dudu coming back, holding two small parcels wrapped in paper. Food. 'Here,' he says, passing us both a wrap. 'The best *cuy* you will find in Iquitos. Enjoy!'

I take the meaty sandwich. It looks a little bit like

KFC. I wonder what *cuy* means – chicken? Pork? I'll look it up in a second, but it smells delicious. 'Thanks, Dudu. I'm starving. We haven't eaten since the plane,' I say. This is what I need, then I'll stop being such a wuss. I'm probably just not feeling like myself because I'm hungry. 'Mmm, delicious!' I mumble through my first mouthful of hot batter and meat. Auntie Marg has a funny smile on her face as she watches me. Maybe I've got mayo on my chin·or something.

I go for a second bite, a big one, and crunch down hard on something . . .

I think it's a bone, so I spit it out into my hand.

It's a claw.

I pull the paper away from the rest of the wrap and open it up. Now I can see what I'm eating. Staring up at me like a cat that's been run over, its arms and legs outstretched as if it's looking for a hug, wrapped in a white floury tortilla blanket . . . is the unmistakable carcass of a guinea pig.

Dear Gav,

Don't expect a lot of contact. We are SOOOOO far away, on the other side of the world, it's practically impossible to get the internet on my phone. I don't want to waste my battery on you anyway. I'm not Skyping you because Mam and Dad don't understand that they don't need to shout to be heard, and it's really awkward.

Just wanted to let you know that I ate a guinea pig today! I wasn't even sick. You could see its claws and little bits of fur, and I think Auntie Marg's one still had an eyeball!!! Don't be freaked out, it's totally normal. Just like we eat cows and chicken, some people here eat guinea pig.

Got to go.

Love
Amy
x

CHAPTER 7

I couldn't sleep last night – the furry faces of our school guinea pigs kept running through my head. I felt really guilty. Especially as it had tasted sooooo good.

We got up at six o'clock this morning, just so Auntie Marg could take pictures of the sun rising. Six o'clock! That's even earlier than on a school day!

Today Auntie Marg is concentrating on taking shots of Iquitos itself, and the people, before we head into the jungle tomorrow.

Dudu's been telling me more about the jungle. He's heard of *el tunchi* and he's suspicious of the pink river dolphin! It's like he really is afraid of the place. The more questions I ask, the more twitchy he gets: 'It's not the size of the snakes you need to worry about, Amy. It's the size of their jaws,' he whispers from behind me as I watch Auntie Marg snapping away at a baby in a woman's arms.

'Why?' I ask, spinning on my heels so that I face him.

'They can dislocate their jaws and swallow things as big as cars. I watched one swallow a cow whole once. It would have gulped you up in seconds,' he says, matter of factly.

I can tell he's searching my face for fear. I show him my Top Trumps cards, the ones Gavin gave me, now stuffed into my plastic pouch with my phone. 'Did it look like this?' I ask, flicking through the cards to the one with a picture of a huge, dark, aggressive-looking anaconda.

Dudu peers at it. '*No! Nothing* like that. The one I saw was *much* bigger,' he says gravely, his words sending a shiver down my spine that I can't hide.

When Gavin tries to tell me the boys at secondary school are going to pierce my ears on the school bus, I know he's exaggerating. But I don't think Dudu is exaggerating. I think he's deadly serious. 'Most of the things that are in the jungle, you won't find in a book or in a little pack of cards!' he goes on. 'The real power, the real strength of the jungle, cannot be captured in this way. There are things, dangerous things, that can't be photographed or explained.' His nose is inches from mine, his voice calm and serious.

'Imagine something, a creature in the water that can cause a strong swimmer to drown!' he continues. 'It is hard to hear them. They are so quiet that you don't know when they are behind you – until it is too late.'

'Who? What's quiet?' I ask.

'*El bufeo colorado.* The pink river dolphins. They are so sneaky, it's hard to know which children they will steal and which they will leave. It's always a surprise,' he says. His eyebrows are raised expectantly and his eyes search my face for a reaction. 'Dangerous, dangerous creatures! A few years ago, a little girl went missing in the jungle and a group of fishermen said they saw a dolphin dive right out of the water and snatch her! She was pulled under the surface, and never seen again.'

I wouldn't be convinced, usually, but there's something in the way he's speaking that makes me feel nervous and there's a hollow feeling in my stomach. 'That's just what you say to scare kids, I bet!' I reply, doing my best to act like I don't care. 'I mean, if you were telling the truth, what do the dolphins do with the children they steal?' I'm not sure I actually want an answer.

'They get turned into dolphins too, and they have to live in the river for ever. The pink dolphins, you see, they were once children, like you. Who walked on these streets. Like you.'

His face is serious, stony, and I try to laugh, but I can't.

'What's all this? You're both looking very serious over here!' says Auntie Marg as she paces towards us, detaching the lens from her camera.

'I am just telling Amy about the pink dolphins. You will not find them anywhere else in the world. Quite unique!' Dudu answers.

'Oh, magnificent!' replies Auntie Marg. 'We must see some! Oh, Dudu, you'll point them out, won't you? We wouldn't want to miss them, would we, Amy!'

'No,' I squeak. My throat feels tight and I'm unable to speak any louder.

Auntie Marg beams at Dudu. 'Such fabulous stories you've been telling us. I can't wait to see it all for myself.'

I get the feeling that wasn't the reaction Dudu was hoping for. As his stories get more gruesome and dangerous, Auntie Marg gets more excited. He keeps scratching his head and looking at her, half baffled, half admiring.

Dudu's brought his son along today too, to help out. Juan is his name. You don't pronounce the 'j', though – you say it as a funny 'h' sound. I said it wrong the first time, but all three of them corrected me in unison, so I won't get it wrong again.

I'm practically fluent in Spanish now. Well, maybe not fluent, but with this app I can work most things out. As long as it's written down, of course. That's probably why Juan seems to be so annoyed with me. Every time I hear a Spanish word that I want to understand, I have to ask Juan to write it down for me, so that I can hover my phone over it. At least I'm trying.

Juan speaks pretty good English, like Dudu, and he's very polite. Mam would love him. 'Can I help you, Margaret? Can I lift that, Margaret?'

67

Apart from that, he's not like Dudu at all. He's very quiet and softly spoken. It's hard to get a proper conversation going – I've been chatting to him all morning, trying to ask him questions, but I'm not getting much back. He has the same dark hair and eyes and olive skin as Dudu, but he's really tall and skinny – almost too tall, because he stoops forward a bit, and he always stands with his left hand behind his back.

He's a year or two older than me, I think. Dudu is a bit bossy with him, but then most dads are, aren't they? Actually, my dad isn't that bossy – my dad is quite funny. Not as funny as he thinks he is, but he can be mildly funny sometimes.

Dudu is making Juan cart Auntie Marg's awkward camera equipment around, including the tripod she puts the camera on. I feel bad for him as there's no way to carry that thing without poking yourself in the head, eye or stomach. But I'm being kept busy too. When Auntie Marg said she could use an assistant, she really meant it. 'Amy, could you help? Amy, batteries. Amy, lens cloth, please. Amy, water, please? Amy . . . Amy . . . Amy!'

I've handed her the wrong piece of equipment

a couple of times and I almost dropped a really expensive lens, but Auntie Marg is so focused, so swept up in everything around her, she hasn't seemed to notice. 'Amy, stand here and look at this composition. Do you see the frame? The light?' She explains how she's set it all up and gestures for me to look through the lens before she clicks the shutter. Her subject is a toothy old man sitting in an armchair on his porch, staring intensely at us.

'Such sadness in his eyes,' she explains. 'The depth and darkness of his wrinkles – it tells a story, don't you think, darling?'

Luckily she has already got Dudu to ask the man's permission to be photographed, otherwise this would be really awkward. 'He's not deaf, Auntie Marg,' I whisper. 'If I talk about Mam's wrinkles she goes nuts. Don't you think he might be a bit offended?!'

She ignores me. '*Gracias, señor*,' she says to the man, who nods.

This is getting boring. We've been taking photos for hours now! Auntie Marg is taking this all *very* seriously. 'Look, Auntie Marg!' I call, deciding I'll liven things up a bit. 'If I run over here, and you hold your hand up in front of that man, palm up, and I take a picture with my phone, we can make it look like he's a tiny man sitting on your hand! It's like that perspective thing you taught me earlier, remember?'

Unamused, she shakes her head. Oh well. Juan might play along. 'Juan!' I call.

Juan looks reluctant, but walks towards me. I reach for his arm to pull it from behind his back. 'Juan, hold up your . . . Oh.' Now I can see his other hand I realize it's broken in some way. Damaged. 'What happened?' I ask, turning it over in front of my face so that I can see both sides. It's as if his hand has been melted. The thumb and the first finger are crooked and look as though they've been welded together, the skin stretched right over them. His other fingers on that hand don't move much either. 'What happened?' I repeat when Juan doesn't answer.

Auntie Marg's head of red, frizzy hair turns towards me. 'Amy, don't ask personal questions!' I didn't know Auntie Marg could frown like Mam, but she's clearly been practising.

Juan totally sees her and just looks at the ground. Awkward.

'Sorry,' I offer, and change the subject quickly. 'So . . . are you on school holidays too?'

Juan nods, but doesn't seem like he's going to share anything else. Wow – this is hard work. 'What do you do in the holidays, then?' I try. 'Have friends over? My brother Gavin's friends pretty much move into our house over the summer holidays. My friends aren't allowed now, though. We let the handbrake off Rebecca's dad's Range Rover when he came to pick her up. It smashed into a wall. It was a write-off.'

Juan looks at me, confused.

'You know! Those massive cars, four by fours.' He still looks confused, so I carry on. 'It wasn't really our fault. Her dad went in to talk to my dad, and we were sitting in the front seats pretending to take our dolls to school . . .' Suddenly a smirk appears on Juan's face and I realize what I've said. 'It was ages ago! We were really little!' I add hastily. 'Anyway, we let the handbrake off. That's what you do when you start a car. Only it was parked on a hill. It started to move. Slowly at first but then, well, then it sort of gathered a bit of speed . . .'

'What happened?' Juan asks, his eyes creeping from the ground towards mine.

'We jumped out,' I tell him. 'We didn't know what else to do, so we just abandoned ship and the rest – well, the car, the wall and an apple tree, they're history. It was a totally innocent mistake. That was the last time I was allowed to have anyone over and the moral of the story is, don't play with dolls.'

Juan still doesn't say anything, but I think I can see the hint of a smile on his face. I see him looking at the cards in the pack around my neck, so I pull them out and show them to him. The one on the top is a vicious-looking scorpion.

'We say *escorpión*,' Juan tells me.

'Very, very dangerous creatures!' Dudu calls. 'Very painful sting! They are everywhere in the jungle. Everywhere you turn!'

'So we're sure to see one,' Auntie Marg says, without taking her eye from the eyepiece.

I swallow. This is feeling like even more of a bad idea, but Auntie Marg's lapping it up.

It's funny – Dudu's our guide while we're here, and he's supposed to be helping us, but it's almost like he's trying to put us off going into the jungle. Why would he do that?

CHAPTER 8

'I've got some beauties this morning! The magazine will love these!' Auntie Marg beams, patting her camera and stepping away from the dusty kids she's been taking photos of.

She had hardly mentioned the magazine or the potential book deal when we were packing – almost as if by talking about it, she might jinx it. So now I can tell she's starting to relax and enjoy herself. It's nice. She looks younger, somehow. She seems happy. 'Now, let's head to another area of town for a few more texture shots and then we'll try some more local delicacies for lunch! What's good here, Dudu?'

'*Ceviche!*' declares Dudu, licking his lips.

'What is that?' I ask, still feeling guilty after yesterday's snack.

'Fish,' explains Juan. 'It is raw, but you squeeze lemon on it to cook it.'

'I bet that's horrible!' I reply, images of Morrison's fish counter in my head.

Marg and Dudu are already wandering ahead, back to the tuk-tuk. Juan shakes his head at me. '*Ceviche* is good. I eat it all the time with my family. It is the—' Juan stops, and his eyes shoot to Dudu, as if checking he is out of earshot.

'I thought you didn't have a family? I thought it was just you and your dad?' I ask curiously. That's what Dudu told Auntie Marg and me this morning. 'But you must have other family *somewhere*,' I continue.

Juan's face is stony. 'It is *not* your business,' he snaps, and marches after Auntie Marg and Dudu. What did I say?!

Fine. I won't ask. Right, where's this food? I jog to catch up with them and we jump back in the tuk-tuk, Auntie Marg and Dudu in the front, me and Juan in the back. Juan's not looking at me, so I ignore him too. We set off, turn a corner and I gasp out loud as a slice of silver appears through the gap in the houses ahead of us.

'The river!' I scramble forward, poking my head between Auntie Marg and Dudu. 'Is that it? Is that the brown sludgy thing we saw from the sky? It's even bigger than I thought!'

There are fewer houses in this part of town, and instead there are rows of shops, all facing the river, their goods spilling onto the street that leads to *el río*. Only it doesn't look like a river at all – it looks like the sea. I can't see the other side. It's so bright that it's like a huge mirror laid out in front of us; with the sun high and bright in the sky it's impossible to see anything other than silhouettes of people on the water's edge, gathered around boats, boxes and crates. Some of them are loading and unloading, some of them are talking, others shouting, but no one is still.

Auntie Marg is snapping away from her seat in the front. The tuk-tuk's so noisy I'm sure I can speak to Juan without either Dudu or Auntie Marg overhearing. I lean across and whisper, 'Juan, why does your dad seem so scared of the jungle? I thought he was winding us up, but when he talks about the jungle he goes a bit weird. His shoulders tense, his hands clench. It's like he's trying to scare us out of it.'

Silence. Juan takes a deep breath. His chest rises and falls. 'You would be scared of the jungle if you were my dad.' His words are slow and pronounced. I can tell he's serious. 'You *should* be scared of it.'

'Why?' I press.

He's silent again, his mouth twitching as if he wants to say something, but isn't sure how.

'Me and Auntie Marg are going to take pictures in there, you know,' I tell him, trying to encourage him to speak.

Juan hesitates, then shakes his head softly. 'It's not a good idea,' he says. 'I would not recommend it. People like you and your aunt, you don't know what you're doing in there. You will just get in the way and make it more— Well, it's not your business.' He stops himself, turning away.

'What's that supposed to mean, *people like you and your aunt*?' I ask, offended. 'What's not my business?'

'You have *no* idea,' he tells me, quietly, seriously. 'It's not a playground in there. It's more dangerous than you know . . .'

His voice trails off as he slumps back into the seat and turns away from me. Dudu brings the tuk-tuk to a halt, turns the key and the vibrating leather seat stops shaking. Auntie Marg leaps out, unscrewing the lens cap on another camera and aiming it in the direction of the river and the industry taking place on its banks. Dudu unfolds his legs from the little vehicle and sets off behind her, calling over his shoulder, '*Quédense aquí con el kit!*' throwing one arm in the air as he goes.

'What did he say?' I turn to Juan.

'Stay here with the kit,' Juan answers, his eyes trained on the water, scanning the shoreline – for what, I am not sure.

I've had enough of him sulking and freezing me out. 'I'm not staying here with you. I'm meant to help!' I tell him. 'There's a lot riding on this, Juan. You won't understand, but Auntie Marg could get a *big* magazine deal out of this. If she does she'll get loads of money and we will celebrate. You won't be invited because we'll probably have the party in London, somewhere posh.' I feel bitter at him for patronising me. I jump out of the tuk-tuk and grab a handful of bits and pieces, confident I've put Juan in his place. Who does he think he is? 'Auntie Marg, do you need another lens?' I shout as I follow her to where she's standing by the water, her camera pointing at a boat full of people like a hunter closing in on prey. 'Auntie Marg?'

She's standing very still, lining up her shot, muttering under her breath, 'Perfect action shot . . . so natural . . .'

The people on the boat all have serious expressions and they're looking to the side, not directly at us, so I call, 'Hey! Smile!' I wave my hands until they notice me. 'Smile!' I call again, pointing at Auntie Marg and her camera.

They frown and turn away, looking wary. Auntie Marg turns on me. 'Amy! Look what you've done! You've ruined it!' she barks angrily. 'That wasn't supposed to be a posed photograph. I didn't want them smiling happily – I wanted to catch them naturally!'

'I was only trying to—' I protest, but I can't get a word in edgeways.

'Go back to the tuk-tuk,' she tells me firmly. 'Honestly, you're being a real nuisance right now.'

She nagged me to help her all morning, and now

she's telling me not to help! I turn my back and head towards the tuk-tuk and Juan is there, a little smirk on his face. I could slap it! I may as well have brought Gav if I had known I'd have to deal with Juan. They are as bad as each other.

Plus, I'm not sure I like this new Auntie Marg. She was a lot nicer when she was floating around her caravan with a cup of herbal tea. *She* was the one who wanted me to come with *her*! I wish Bob was here, he never gets upset with me. I never offend him. A good furry, slobbery cuddle from my four-legged friend would be perfect right now. But he's hundreds of miles away, with Mam and Dad. I never miss home, but I think I do right now. Just a tiny bit. Well, not home. Just Bob.

Arriving at the tuk-tuk, I give it a good kick. (It hurt more than I thought, but I won't show it!) Slumping into the driver's seat, the anger bubbles in the back of my throat. The tears threatening, I throw my head onto the steering wheel to stop Juan from seeing my red, embarrassed face, and my shoulder catches something.

Chug, chug . . .

The engine is on. Two breaths from the little engine is all I get as warning before the tuk-tuk leaps forward. I've knocked the ignition switch!

Juan springs out of the back seat as I throw my hands on the wheel to try and take control. I spin to see where he's landed, which means I accidentally throw the wheel to the left, sending this speedy tin can on wheels lurching to the side. Now I'm hurtling forward. Auntie Marg has her back to me, and I'm heading straight for her!

Dudu dives out of the way too, yelling, '*Atención! Atención!*' and waving his arms at Auntie Marg, but she's wrapped up in taking her pictures. She has no idea I'm coming. I'm frozen with fear – I can't stop it! Knowing what's about to happen, I throw myself from the driver's seat. The little vehicle ploughs straight into my auntie and then into the shop behind her, with flip-flops, knives, postcards and bags of nuts exploding in the air.

I can't see Auntie Marg as I watch the little vehicle of mass destruction pile into the shop. The tuk-tuk crumples like an empty packet of crisps. The cracked leather seats are swallowed up by the metal frame.

The engine squeals, then stops, as rips, the sound of breaking glass and a gigantic thud fill the air.

The cloud of dust whipped up by the accelerating tuk-tuk is starting to settle and clear, but I still can't see Auntie Marg. Dudu is on his feet, shoulders square and hands clenched. The tripod, the camera lens and the batteries are scattered among the rubble, as if Auntie Marg's kit bag has exploded. Wait – is that the camera that was around her neck? The one now hanging from a sign next door?

But where is Auntie Marg . . . ?

Dear Gav,

Things have been pretty busy here. Auntie
Marg has taken so many photos already that
she's going to have a few days off. Nothing
to worry about. She's fine. Well, she will be.
Hopefully. There was a teeny little crash
involving Auntie Marg and a tuk-tuk (which is a
sort of taxi) but don't tell Mam I said that. The
most important thing is that it wasn't my fault. At
all. Don't tell Mam I said that either.

Actually, DELETE THIS EMAIL, GAV.

Amy
x

CHAPTER 9

'*Ayúdenla! Ayúdenla!*'

Dudu yells over the chaos. People pick through the rubble, peeling back bent tin and morning goods from the shops cluttering the crash scene. It's only one little tuk-tuk, but it looks like a bulldozer's made this mess! He's interrupted by bloodcurdling screams: 'Aeeooghhhhhowwwwwww!' I've never actually known what 'bloodcurdling' meant, but I think this qualifies. I know it's Auntie Marg, because in between the screams I can hear her trying to say, 'Darlings!'

It's awful. I want her to stop, but each time someone lifts a bucket or a piece of wood away from her, she screams some more. One arm seems to be pointing the wrong way but it's hard to tell. People are helping her, but I can't – I can't move.

I'm glued to the spot as I watch the chaos continue.

Dudu peels away from the melee and is heading towards me. '*Qué chica más tonta e irresponsable!*' He spits the words out, the veins in his neck and eyes bulging, angry and red. I want to run but I can't.

Dudu grabs me, his sweaty hand heavy on my arm. My knees buckle. He's shaking me and shouting, '*Usted pudo haberla matado! Mire el daño!*'

I don't know what he's saying but from his furious face I know it's not good.

There's no choice: I spin into Dudu, whipping his face with my long hair, putting my back against his front, raising my knee so I can scour my Converse-clad heel right down his shin. He yelps and lets go, and I am off, throwing my arms and my legs forward, propelling myself along the dusty pavement, dodging the confused crowd.

One kid goes flying and a woman yells – but I can't help it and I can't stop. I daren't. The blood is pumping through my veins so fast all I can hear is a thudding sound in my ears.

Finally, when I can no longer hear Dudu yelling behind me, I stop; only for a second, to turn and make sure that he's not chasing me. The water's now a distant silver sliver on the horizon. I'm surrounded by houses, washing lines and porches packed with people in the dustiest part of town. That's the fastest I've ever run – even Gav would be impressed with that speed.

My chest rises and falls dramatically as my body tries to take in enough air to catch my breath and calm my chaotic thoughts. What have I done? Have I killed Auntie Marg? I was cross with her but I didn't want to do that! Will anyone believe me? What are Mam and Dad going to say? What will we do without her? Regret and panic pulsate through my body, my fingernails digging into my palms as I clench my fists, panicking, scared, alone.

She didn't *sound* dead, but she might still die. People die after accidents all the time. They *will* take her to hospital, won't they? What's Spanish for hospital? I didn't hear anyone say anything that sounded like hospital, but then I couldn't hear much through Dudu's ranting and those awful wails from Auntie Marg.

Thinking of the crash and the chaos sends a shiver

down my spine. The look on Dudu's face swims through my head, angry and shocked. Shocked that I could be so stupid. I *am* stupid! I wanted to prove Mam and Dad and Gav wrong on this trip. I wanted to show them I'm not a disaster, but I am. I might be a murderer. I ruined Dudu's tuk-tuk and the shop and made a scene in front of the WHOLE street.

It wasn't really all my fault, was it? That flipping son of his *could* have helped. But *no*, he bailed. Jumped out of the tuk-tuk as soon as it started moving forward. Such a boy, letting me take all the blame. *He'll* probably be saying it's all my fault, no doubt. He clearly didn't like me anyway, even before this.

Think. What do I do?

Poor Auntie Marg. I really, really hope she's OK . . .

'Juan! *Por aquí!*'

Dudu's voice! I peer around the corner and see him and Juan running down the dusty street.

I need to run. I need to get out of here.

The houses around me are close together, almost spilling into one another, the paths in between them narrow and rambling, most of them lined with clean washing on outstretched washing lines. A white sheet pinned by its corners is blocking one of the pathways and I consider it as my escape route momentarily, but my muscles freeze with fear as an unmistakable shadow moves across the sheet.

It's thrown back and Dudu is staring at me.

'*Allí está!*' cries Juan from behind me.

With every bit of strength I can muster, I propel myself forward towards a porch peppered with swinging chairs. An old man is sitting in one, staring straight at me. His eyes widen and his mouth falls open as I throw myself into a chair and scramble onto the wooden railings that frame their home. A lady in the doorway is clapping as my hands cling onto the hot tin roof. Wriggling my legs to get the momentum I need to swing my body up, I can hear her laughing.

The sharp edge of the roof scrapes my shin as I pull my entire body up and roll onto my back for a second. Like a fish being laid onto a barbecue, I swear I can hear myself sizzle as my calves rest against the hot tin momentarily.

BOOM!

I peep over the edge and see that Dudu has

grabbed a broom and is on the porch, thumping the underside of the roof. Before he breaks a hole in it, I'm off, galloping across the patchwork of roof tops. The houses here are so close together, laid out in a grid-like fashion. Like at home when I'm on the barn roof (when I *used* to go on the barn roof), I can see where people are heading – but Dudu and Juan can't see me. My thunderous footsteps on the tin roofs are confusing them.

Until I know Auntie Marg is OK, or I can find a way to go home, I have to keep out of Dudu's way. I can't stay up here for long, though – I feel like the human equivalent of a sausage in a pan, it's *so* hot. I need to get down soon, and there's only one place Dudu won't look for me. He's made it clear he hates the river. He's done nothing but try to scare us out of going on the water since we got here! There may be some dangers, but could anything be more dangerous than Dudu right now?

Maybe.

Dear Gav,

Sending this email from my phone. I need your brain . . . Can you remember how we made a tent that night Mam let us sleep down by the river? Don't tell Mam, but I kind of need one now and I can't remember what we used. Or did Mam get us out from our sleeping bags and make us sleep in the car? Either way, any ideas useful. Thanks.

Amy
x

PS. Just asking out of interest. We have a hotel, obviously.
PPS. If you could treat this email as a matter of urgency that would be great. It's not urgent, it's just a question, but email me now please.
PPPS. I think it's important you all know that I am very fond of you all and I would never intentionally hurt any of you. Well, I hurt YOU sometimes, but I would never kill any of you, is what I mean.

CHAPTER 10

I kind of wish I hadn't sent Gav that email now. It made me miss home. Gav is quite good at dens, though, and I could do with a den now.

I stayed on the rooftops for as long as I could. It's lucky I have such long hair as it's the only shade and protection I had from the sun all afternoon. I sat huddled on that tin for hours, hiding under my hair, until it went dark and it felt safe to crawl down and make for the riverside. My head's pounding and my mouth's dry. I haven't had anything to drink since this morning.

I'm pretty confident he won't come to the water's edge. I waited until dark, dodging between the street lights, staying in shadows in case Dudu was lurking somewhere, but he won't come here. The water's black, the ferry workers left hours ago.

There must be at least fifteen jetties in a row, some wood and some concrete, each with ten or twelve boats tied to them.

There's one at the end with *Anna Maria* written in white swirly writing down the side. It's small, so I can see there's no one on board, so I'll go with that one. Plus, it looks old and unused, which is perfect. No fisherman or potential friend of Dudu's to find me at 5 a.m.

I climb in. I'll get some sleep in here. I am soooo tired. I'll work out what to do tomorrow. I think I'm still suffering a bit of that jet lag. All I need to do is get rid of these bags, whatever they are, and make a bit of room for myself. These petrol cans don't really make good pillows, so I'll put them on the side of the jetty too. But the bottles of water . . . what a lifesaver! I slurp down a bottle and half of another, then snuggle into as tight a ball as I can manage, shuffling down underneath the plastic cover that stretches across the boat.

The boat rocks very gently and I close my eyes . . .

* * *

I wake up to a thudding noise and the movement of the boat swaying from side to side. My eyes feel like they are stuck together and I'm still half asleep, my legs knotted and sore from my awkward sleeping position, but there is no denying it. I'm awake.

It's late morning. I must have slept for *hours*.

There is someone else on this boat.

We're moving!

How did this happen? This was the boat that looked the least likely to go anywhere! What if they're pirates? There are real pirates in this part of the world, only they steal boats, not kids. I think.

What if someone saw me get in, and now they're kidnapping me? No – surely if they were *intentionally* kidnapping me, they would have tied me up? They must not have realized I was here, hiding under the blue plastic sheet at this end of the boat. But where are we going? What do I do? Keep my head down? Stay hidden or reveal myself?

Too late – my decision's been made for me. The plastic sheeting over my head is rustling. Whoever is on the other side of it is moving it, chinks of light are breaking through the gaps, stinging my eyes. A flood of white light hits me in the face as the sheet is pulled back. A solitary silhouette is standing over me, a skinny figure against the sun with one hand tucked behind its back.

'What are *you* doing here?' Juan and I yell in unison.

I stagger to my feet, my legs numb from the way I slept. I want to eyeball him, nose to nose like boxers do, but he's too tall. 'What are you doing here?' I repeat. The last person I wanted to see today is him. (Well, actually he's the second to last. The worst person would be Dudu.)

Juan stares at me in disbelief. 'This is *my boat*!' he tells me. 'We were looking for you all day yesterday and this is where you were hiding all along?' He lets out a furious torrent of Spanish and I would put money on some of those words being swear words.

'Actually, I was hiding on a rooftop for most of yesterday, and I didn't know it was your boat!' I shoot back.

Juan makes a sound that's half sigh, half frustrated growl and grabs his hair with his hands. 'I have to take you back,' he tells me, turning and throwing himself down at the rudder.

'*No!*' I cry, panicking. 'Not yet! Please, Juan. Your dad was so angry and they'll probably throw me in prison and I'll have to eat guinea pig and raw fish every day! And my mam will be raging, and there'll be no one to take Bob on proper long walks . . . please don't take me back yet. I just need a bit of time for everything to calm down.'

He shakes his head firmly. 'No. You must go back right away. I have things to take care of. You cannot be here! I can't believe I have wasted the last three hours travelling in one direction and now I will have to turn around and start again!'

'Three hours?' I can't believe I slept through that. 'Just think about it, Juan – if you let me stay, you can just carry on with your journey and you won't have wasted all that time. I'll sit here quietly, and I won't say a word. You won't even know I'm here.'

He's silent for a minute, then he sighs angrily. 'Fine. But I have things to do, Amy. You have to stay quiet and do what I tell you, and don't ask questions. Especially not about where we are going, OK?'

'Why, where *are* we going?' I ask, intrigued, then I correct myself. 'I mean . . . where we're going is *none* of my business. Got it.'

Surely he won't be going far. A day trip into the jungle. That'll be enough time for Dudu to calm down.

'I might put you on a boat going back to Iquitos before we get that far . . .' Juan mutters to himself.

Wriggling out from underneath the plastic sheet, I perch on an upturned bucket, facing the mighty waterway. Ginormous trees line our route and cast a strange green glow onto the water. I sit quietly and try not to ask questions – for a moment, anyway.

'Juan . . . how's my auntie?' I ask nervously, not sure if I want to hear the answer.

'Not great,' he replies flatly. 'She is in hospital.'

I don't know where to look. I feel awful. In hospital. *I* put her in hospital. I feel sick.

'She's alive, though,' I say, reassuring myself and smiling at Juan, and praying for a smile back. If he smiles, that's good, right? It's going to be OK.

Nothing. No smile. I wish this wasn't happening.

I change the subject to try and distract myself;

anything to stop the wave of guilt creeping over my body.

'I didn't know you had a boat, Juan,' I try. 'Does anyone else use it? Is it hard to drive with your bad hand? Does your dad know you're out here? How far are we going?'

Juan grits his teeth angrily. He's annoyed. He is *not* happy.

CHAPTER 11

Juan hasn't found a boat going the other way to put me on. Not yet, anyway. By early evening, we must have passed ten boats sailing in the opposite direction to us, most of them bigger than ours, some with crowds of people on board and rows of bright hammocks. One boat we passed was carrying an entire herd of cows! I knew Gavin wouldn't believe me, so I slid my phone into camera mode and took photos of each one.

The crowds on the riverside seem more distant along this part of the river. As we pass what I am guessing are towns – collections of white buildings with tin roofs – there are loads of people buzzing around boats of all shapes, sizes and colours as boxes, crates and animals are transferred from the water to the ground and back again. I snap picture after picture. I don't even need to put any special filters or effects on the photos – it looks like something from one of Auntie Marg's books or magazines already.

For the first time since arriving in Iquitos, I feel a breeze. We're not going fast, but fast enough for me to appreciate the cool air on my hot, sticky face. The noise of the crowds on the shore is now replaced by a whirr from the engine and the rhythmical splashing against the boat as we cut through the dark, thick water. I can't move, I don't want to take myself out of the breeze – it's amazing, wonderful, and it takes away the soggy sweaty feeling that cocoons you all day in Iquitos.

It's getting towards evening now, but the sun is still in the sky, not high enough to burn my forehead and arms, but high enough to make everything feel summery. Golden.

If it's sunny at home, Gavin will probably camp in the garden tonight. His mates will probably be allowed to stay too, and I bet they'll have a barbecue.

If I've seriously hurt Auntie Marg, they might put

me up for adoption and let Jack or Billy move in. I'd hate them to give up my room.

I didn't *mean* to hurt Auntie Marg. Maybe if I send Gav a photo and keep in touch by email, they'll know I love them, and they'll know I wouldn't do anything to hurt Auntie Marg on purpose.

'Juan, is there wifi anywhere? Is there a hot spot I can get onto? I just want to give my family a quick call, or send my brother an email or a Facebook message . . .'

Juan stares at me in disbelief. His eyebrows are raised so high they've practically disappeared into his hairline. 'Wifi?' he repeats. 'The internet cafe is back in Iquitos, in the hotel. You can swim back there if you wish – don't let me stop you.'

He's acting like I'm stupid. My actual friends wouldn't think that was a stupid question. You can *always* find wifi somewhere – everyone knows that. 'You're just jealous because your phone doesn't even take photos,' I say. 'It's like the one my grandad has – all it does is send texts! I'll let you use mine if you don't waste the battery and you help me find wifi, though.'

'Amy, there *is* no wifi around here. At all. No shop. No road. No town. No village for *miles*,' he says. 'Look around you. There is *no* way to get in touch with anybody out here. If you want to see or speak to people, you go and see them. Face to face.'

'What about Auntie Marg? How will we know if . . . well, you know, if . . .' I can't get the words out. 'Is there any way we can find out whether she'll be OK?' I ask the question feeling like someone has punched me in the stomach.

Juan's gaze dips and he shrugs his shoulders. 'Maybe.'

'Where are we ACTUALLY going, Juan? Will there be a phone there? Maybe we could ask them to—'

'NO. They don't. Where we're going, they DON'T have a phone to call Iquitos. They don't WANT to call Iquitos, OK?'

I stare at him. His face is flushed. Well, *that* was an overreaction. I was only asking. We sit in silence.

Well, I can still use my phone to take photos, even if I can't do very much else with it. I just took one of a massive lily pad. Seriously, it was almost as big as this boat! It looked like it had tiny frogs living on it, but it's hard to see in this fading light. I'll zoom in on the photo and find out once I get home. Not now, though – I don't want to waste the battery. I'll write emails to Gav and just save them in my drafts folder, so I'm keeping a sort of record of the trip. I'll turn it off in between.

This is good, actually – not having any signal or internet out here. If I can't email or call my family, I can't miss them. Plus, Mam might have asked to speak to Auntie Marg, and I'd have had to pretend she was busy or in the bath or something, and my voice might give something away.

What if Auntie Marg's already contacted home from the hospital? Told Mam and Dad about the accident, told them I've disappeared?

Don't think about that. *Don't think about it.*

No phone calls also means I won't know if they're having a barbecue, therefore I won't care. I would *love* a burger. Now it's getting cooler – it's far too hot to eat in the middle of the day – I'm *starving*. I wonder what we'll eat? I haven't seen anything on the boat yet, but my belly's rumbling now. I'm getting really thirsty as well – I've finished the bottles of water on board. For the first time, I realize I don't have anything with me apart from my phone.

No passport – that's back in the hotel room with Auntie Marg's.

No money, not that I'd be able to spend it anywhere on the river.

No spare clothes, no sun cream (Mam would kill me, she's obsessed about us wearing sun cream). No hair bands, cherryade or chocolate, either.

I have my cards in the pouch around my neck – the Top Trumps ones.

'Hey, Juan, let's have a game!' I shuffle the cards, deal them into two piles and thrust one of the piles at him. He doesn't take it, so I place the pile next to him. 'Go on, pick one!' I urge.

Nothing. Juan isn't getting involved.

'Fine, I'll go first,' I tell him, and turn over the top card on my pile. I was expecting something like a jaguar or a caiman, but the image on the card shows a slender, shadowy figure. '*Saci pererê,*' I read slowly. 'Juan, am I pronouncing that right? *A young prankster believed to cause mischief and chaos in the Amazon jungle* . . . This is cool, Juan! Have you ever heard of this *Saci pererê* before? Apparently, there is a myth that' – I put on a spooky, mysterious voice to read out the next bit – '*a young boy who suffered pain and heartbreak at the hands of the jungle gets his own back by causing—*'

Juan snatches the phone from my hands and sends my deck of cards flying. 'Careful!' I yell. 'What's wrong with you?'

'Why did you do that stupid voice? *Saci pererê* is not a *ghost*!' Juan snaps.

'Give that back. My mam bought me that!' I insist, reaching for the phone.

'Fine!' Juan throws it at me.

'Well, that was childish,' I say, tucking it back in the pouch around my neck and bending down to scoop up the cards that are scattered by my feet. 'Are you going to explain what I said to make you flip out like that? All I was doing was reading something out loud!' I look at him curiously. 'You're not scared, are you? Of the things my cards say live out here?' I put my mysterious voice back on, knowing it will annoy him. '*The dense forest all around us . . . no shops or villages or grown-ups to protect us . . .'*

'You don't know what you are talking about,' he snaps.

For the next twenty minutes he full-on ignores me, staring straight ahead. I try asking questions. I try being nice. I try being rude. Nothing works. Then I hear his belly rumbling too, and I realize he's probably just as hungry as I am.

'Any food, Juan?' I ask hopefully. 'Or water?'

Juan hesitates for a moment, then turns to me and nods – though I can tell it's reluctantly. 'Yes. We should eat. There are some bottles of water and some sandwiches in a pack under there,' he tells me, nodding at the blue plastic sheet that lies bunched up by my feet. 'By the spare petrol. Get that out as well. We'll need some more for the engine soon.'

'Under here?' I ask, rummaging around. Something's niggling at my brain. A pack . . . spare petrol . . .

Juan nods again. 'Yes, it's all there. I always get the boat ready a day or two before a trip.'

And suddenly I remember throwing things out of the boat onto the jetty to make room for myself to hide.

Uh-oh.

SACI PERERÊ

A young prankster believed to cause mischief and chaos in the Amazon jungle. Fast and able, Saci is able to disappear at a moment's notice. It is rumoured that a young boy who suffered pain and heartbreak now gets his own back by causing problems for anyone who is hurting the jungle.

Appearance:

Because he appears and disappears so quickly, there are conflicting descriptions. Most stories suggest Saci only has one leg. Others say he has two legs but one arm. All say he has holes in the palms of his hands and can hold and play with fire, allowing the embers to fall through the holes.

Top strength:

He is agile, strong and always gets the better of his enemies. Despite his mischievous behaviour, he is known as a force for good.

Most likely to be found:

Impossible to say! Most stories come from Brazilian parts of the Amazon, but he doesn't seem loyal to any one part of the rainforest.

Deadly?

No. Saci may torment and tease youngsters by hiding their toys, but he means no real harm, and only really disrupts the lives of people who deserve it.

SCARE RATING: 21 • DANGER RATING: 39 • COOL RATING: 88

CHAPTER 12

'You can pick the first Top Trump?' I offer.

'That looks like a nice tree?' I go on.

'Do you think that's a sloth?' I ask.

I'm desperately trying to break the silence. When Juan realized I had taken his supplies out of the boat so that I could be a stowaway, and guzzled down all his water, he was pretty miffed. I'm trying to make the situation better by chattering away to him. He's got to forgive me at some point, right?

But hours must have passed and he hasn't said a word to me.

It's getting dark. The constant stream of boats has slowed, but not stopped altogether. My favourites are the huge ferries carrying what must be hundreds of passengers, each level decorated with rows and rows of brightly coloured hammocks and dozens of people hanging over the sides. 'Where are they all going?' I ask.

Juan sighs, obviously deciding it's easier to answer me than keep pretending I don't exist. 'To the next town. Or the one after that,' he says. 'The men move around for work and their families can be spread all over. Some men have two or even three different families.'

'More than one family? Don't their wives go mad?' I ask.

'They never see each other,' he explains. 'Each family stays in one place all the time, so they would never know.'

'Like your dad,' I realize. 'He stays in Iquitos all the time, doesn't he? And he really didn't want to go into the jungle with me and Auntie Marg, even though he was supposed to be our guide all through the trip.' I guess in a way I solved that problem for him. 'Why, though?' I ask. 'Is he *really* scared of the river, or were you both trying to wind me up?'

Juan sighs. 'Yes, he is scared. But not of this part of the river. This part is crazy, but not scary. Crazy with people and ships and boats from sunrise to sunfall. It's what's *beyond* this bit that scares him. Everything that happens off the main river and in the jungle.'

'What *is* in the jungle?' I ask, curious to know which of the stories I've heard are true. 'There are loads of stories and myths about this part of the world. Auntie Marg wanted to take photos to try and capture the mystery of it. You know – piercing eyes, powerful trees. She was pretty excited about coming here.' I realize there's excitement in my voice, too. In spite of the situation I'm in, this place *is* pretty awesome. Everything is so big. Even the birds above us are massive, with flaming red wings and navy flashes.

'No one knows everything about the jungle. No one knows exactly,' Juan says. 'I know what I would *like* there to be . . .' His voice trails off.

'What do you mean, you know what you would *like* there to be?' I ask, puzzled. For a minute I wonder if he's going to describe some wild, colourful creature, and I start flicking through the Top Trumps cards again, wondering which of them he's going to mention.

'I'd like us all to be back there,' Juan says. 'My family. We all lived there together.' He pauses. 'Until the accident,' he adds.

'Hang on,' I say, looking up from my cards. 'What accident?'

Juan's face is tight and stern. His eyes glance at his withered hand. My eyes follow and stay there a little longer. The skin is so strikingly white compared to his tanned arms and legs; the flesh stretched and twisted over his knuckles. He can see me staring, but I can't take my eyes off it.

'I don't want to talk about it,' he says quietly. Now is the time to bite my lip. I've asked him questions and he gets his knickers in a knot. I don't want to upset him. But I'm desperate to know. I'm desperate to hear more about Juan's family, too – he and Dudu said that it was just the two of them, but that's obviously not true.

'Juan, why didn't you tell me and Auntie Marg that you were planning on travelling into the jungle today?' I ask, careful not to mention his family for fear of upsetting him. 'We were talking about it before. I said we wanted to travel into the jungle. You could have just mentioned it. Instead you listened to your dad trying to scare us.'

Juan looks at me. 'Why do you think I did not mention it?' he asks. 'I knew if I did, you would want to come with me.'

'Isn't that kind of selfish?' I ask.

Juan snorts. 'Selfish!' he repeats. '*Me*, selfish? Look at you, Amy. You were here to help your aunt, and see what happened. You didn't help – you just caused trouble. Don't talk to me about being selfish. I have things to do – important things. Things that are nothing to do with you.'

I didn't mean it to come out like that. 'That's not fair. I *did* help Auntie Marg. At least, I *tried* to help. I was just starting to get the hang of remembering which lens was which. If things hadn't gone so wrong with the tuk-tuk, Auntie Marg would be taking the photos of her life right now and it would be partly down to me!'

My protests fall on deaf ears. Juan has his back to me now, studying the engine. His fiddling is punctuated by chugs and clicks.

'And now we are running out of fuel,' Juan mutters.

'When we do, I will have to paddle. So we will move slowly.' He looks sharply at me. 'You didn't throw the paddle out too, did you?'

I bite my lip. 'No! Of course not.' I'm looking around in the bottom of the boat, frantically racking my brain. Did I throw it out to make room? Oh, please don't let me have done that!

'Here!' I shout, grabbing it. 'See? I would never have thrown *this* out.' I'm patting the paddle as if I had known where it was all along.

Juan snatches the paddle and dunks it in the water. Time to stay quiet.

The atmosphere on board isn't fun, but this place is amazing. It might sound boring, but I've been watching the banking for ages now. It moves all the time. It's so steep, it's like a cliff. Hundreds of tree roots burst through the soil, stretching out over the water like witches' fingers straining to break the surface. Every now and again, huge chunks of chocolate-brown earth fall into the river. The walls of mud that line the water's edge aren't solid – far from it. They crumble as the river eats its way further into the jungle, setting tree roots free, allowing them to stretch out of the mud, straining for the water. When the bigger chunks of earth break off and splash into the water, they cause ripples and throw out small waves that rock our boat from side to side.

Juan is steering us closer to the banking now, towards one of the watery pathways that ebb away from the main flow and into the dense dark jungle.

'What are we going in there for? It looks pretty dark. Juan, are you sure?' I question.

'*Relájese!*' he replies, looking straight ahead. I know that word means *relax*, but he didn't say it in a way that makes me want to relax. He said it in a way that makes me want to hit him.

The nose of our shabby little boat seems to follow his gaze, pointing straight for the jungle, and our pace slows as the river bounces off the side of the boat while we cut across it. The leafy green canopy stretches miles above our heads, tightly packed trees towering over us, and the darkness swallows the boat as Juan steers us into the unknown.

It's so dark, so much darker in here. The thick leaves and branches knit together, blocking the sun and most of the daylight. Here and there, beams of white light pierce the greenery. There's just enough of them to make everything visible – like bright white torches shining down. The water, barely moving here, is much more shallow, and darker too. Creeping towards the front of the boat, I lean over the nose and put my hands beneath the surface. It's so dark they disappear from sight completely, thick clay-like mud between my fingers. There are twigs and leaves, squidgy worms and – well, I'm not entirely sure what *that* is.

Taking my hand quickly from the water, I can feel the crusty shell of something that has latched onto the tip of my finger. It's like a miniature crab, only with a long tail. With my free hand I fumble for my phone, slide it to camera with my thumb and awkwardly take a photo. The creature flinches in the flash and flicks its tail up higher.

Then I realize what it is.

It's a scorpion!

I drop my phone and start to scrabble through the Top Trumps cards next to me with one hand. I'm sure one of them was about scorpions. I'm sure it said that scorpions have poison in their tails, and that if they sting you, it can be *lethal*.

I normally like stuff like this. Slugs? Love them. Spiders? Adore them. Mice and rats are OK too – but scorpions? Scorpions that are attached to your finger? That's a bit different.

Shaking my hand frantically doesn't budge it. Shaking my whole arm doesn't budge it either, until

'*Ouch!*'

I whack my hand on the side of the boat and it falls off, landing back in the water.

'Determined little thing,' I say, trying to make my voice sound casual. My heart's thudding in my chest. *I just had a scorpion stuck to my finger!*

My fingertip is nipped, but not bleeding. Juan, barely batting an eyelid, has – unsurprisingly – *not* reacted. Although there's that annoying hint of a smile back on his face.

Typical.

SCORPION

One of the first animals to live on this planet, scorpions can survive pretty much anywhere and are found all over the world, apart from Antarctica.

Appearance:

They have eight legs, large pincers to catch and injure prey, and their tails – which contain poisonous glands – curl over their bodies. There are thousands of different types, ranging in colour and size. Their bodies are divided into three sections: head, tummy and tail.

Top strength:

Some can survive for a whole year on just one insect. They have amazing metabolisms that can adapt to where they live.

Most likely to be found:

Everywhere! They can survive all over the world and will eat insects, bugs and even small vertebrates.

Deadly?

All scorpions carry poison in their tails and have a stinger to attack prey, but not all are deadly. Even baby scorpions can produce a lot of venom, though, so don't underestimate them!

SCARE RATING: 77 • DANGER RATING: 69 • COOL RATING: 83

CHAPTER 13

Our boat is finally at a standstill. We're wedged into the muddy river bed beneath us, and it feels calm.

The sun fell below the horizon a few hours ago, but out on the main river the heat was still intense. In here, it's intense in a different way. In an energy-sapping way, as if I've been wrapped in a warm wet blanket. I'm damp and sweaty in the suffocating warmth. At least for the first time all day, my skin doesn't feel like it is tightening and crisping. Mam would kill me if she knew how many hours I'd been out without putting more sun cream on.

My ponytail lies heavy on my head, against my neck and shoulders. It's too long for this heat. Maybe Mam was right – maybe I *should* go to the hairdressers more.

The sound of water lapping our boat and the distant chug of engines has been replaced by moans and groans, funny clicks and quacks – from what, I don't know. Different sounds echo through the tree tops. Their trunks stretch miles above our heads. They're taller than the biggest buildings I have ever seen. The shadows creep over each other as a breeze moves the leaves here and there. The dusky light makes it hard to see exactly what's what. I can see Juan's silhouette, his sharp jaw, but his expression is difficult to make out.

Auntie Marg would probably love it in here. It's eerie, that's for sure, and she likes eerie. When there's a full moon on the farm she goes out taking pictures of the mice and rats that scuttle through the barns. She does it all night!

I hope she gets to do that again. I hope she hasn't seen her last rat.

I shiver, looking around as a high-pitched wail echoes above our heads. 'Juan, why have we come in here? And what is that? That sound?' I try to point in the direction of the noise, but I have no idea where it's coming from. I *thought* it was above me, but now

I think it's on my left, coming from the spider's web of twigs and trees. Or is it at the water's edge? The dense green carpet spilling into the river?

'Eooooghahahah!' It's like musical laughter, a creepy shrieking that makes the hair on the back of my neck stand on end, partly due to excitement and partly due to fear.

'Juan,' I hiss, straining my eyes to make shapes from the shadows. 'What's making that noise? It sounds like when one of the farm cats gets stuck on the barn roof. You can hear them, but you can't see them, so you have to climb and crawl, following the noise until you find it and set it free. Do you have cats in the jungle, Juan?' I scan the jungle canopy for movement.

'There are cats in the jungle, but not like your cats. Anyway, THAT is not a cat,' Juan replies. 'And didn't my father tell you about the noises? You can see how it would be easy to get lost in here, can't you?'

Hang on . . . I know where I've heard that noise before. The programme I watched with Auntie Marg and Gav. I shuffle quickly through my Top Trumps cards until I get to the one I'm looking for. *El tunchi.*

'He did try to warn you,' Juan adds, shrugging his shoulders and ignoring my obvious panic.

'Well, I didn't know we were going into the jungle when I jumped into your stupid boat! I was only hiding while your dad calmed down. I didn't mean to end up here! And now we're surrounded by some kind of jungle spirit! I still don't even know where we're going. Please tell me we're heading back to the main river in the morning? We're not staying here, are we?' I think I'd rather face Dudu than deal with this.

'We cannot stay on the main river overnight, Amy,' Juan explains patiently. 'It is too busy. We don't want to be seen by— Well, just trust me, it would be too dangerous.'

'Who don't we want to see us?' I ask nervously. 'You can't just start saying something like that and not finish your sentence! I want to—' A distant screech interrupts me, and we both look straight up to the dense canopy above us, every shade of green above our heads. 'We're definitely moving on in the morning?' I persist, and Juan nods. 'Well, will you at least tell me where we're going and why? I know I promised I wouldn't ask, but I really want to know. The thing is, if we're going near a village or a town, maybe they'll have a phone or a way to contact the hospital back in Iquitos. This stuff is weird, but the thought that maybe I . . .' I struggle to find the words for what I want to say. 'Well, the thought that maybe I hurt Auntie Marg really badly is more terrifying than anything.' I stumble over the last few words, feeling like I've run up a hundred stairs.

Juan hesitates. 'We are going to visit my family,' he says, avoiding eye contact.

I let this sink in for a second. 'What's the deal there?' I ask in my softest voice possible. 'You clearly don't like to talk about it, but if I'm going to meet them, I don't want to put my foot in it . . . I don't want to say the wrong thing.' I'm speaking slowly and carefully, trying my best not to offend or annoy him. 'Why do you and Dudu live in Iquitos if your family live in the jungle?' I continue, riskily, knowing family is a touchy subject.

I've gone too far. The expression on his face is serious. His jaw clenched, he folds his arms under his head and his legs under his awkward body, closes his eyes and ignores me completely.

'I'm achy and sore from sleeping in this boat last night,' I grumble, lying down myself and trying to get comfortable. 'Don't you have any proper—' I was about to say pillows or sheets, but I realize they might have been in the bags that I threw out, so I stop myself. 'If we were camping in our back garden,' I say instead, 'my mam would bring us a drink about now – a hot chocolate with marshmallows, probably. She always does – she pretends she isn't checking up on me and Gav, but we know she is really! It would be nice, though, round about now, wouldn't it? Maybe some biscuits to go with it? She'd even bring us a pillow and blankets if she was here—'

'Well, she's not, so stop talking about it,' Juan cuts in, turning his body away from me and folding his arms. 'Go to sleep.'

Wow – I was only trying to lighten the mood. Make some small talk. Distract us from the hunger, my aching belly, the noises above us and the very real possibility that I might have seriously damaged the only member of my family who gets me.

'Juan,' I whisper. 'I think . . . I'm not sure, but I think the noises are getting louder.'

Juan starts snoring.

I might just hang onto this oar, for now. Just in case.

EL TUNCHI

A spirit that terrorizes people who disrespect the rainforest, announcing its presence with a haunting whistle. *El tunchi* is drawn to people who respond to his whistle.

Appearance:

Exists as a whistle that gets louder and higher in pitch until the person *el tunchi* is targeting repeats the whistle. Once they repeat the whistle *el tunchi* will cause chaos.

Top strength:

Cannot be caught or stopped.

Most likely to be found:

All over the rainforest. Most likely to be heard when on your own, or the only one awake.

Deadly?

No. Mischievous and problematic. *El tunchi* will have its fun and teach people a lesson.

SCARE RATING: 31 • DANGER RATING: 33 • COOL RATING: 79

Dear Gavin,

Short email, because we are doing too much
cool stuff for me to spend time writing to you.
Just to let you know that TV programme was
right. *El tunchi* does exist! I heard it. You would
be scared. You wouldn't like it.

Love you. Sort of.
Amy
x

PS. I haven't had to brush my teeth for what
feels like days.
PPS. I have no signal at the moment, so by the
time you get this email I will probably be back
home, but in case anything happens to me, in
case I get arrested, for instance – sometimes
that happens to TOTALLY innocent people – I
just wanted you to have a record of what an
excellent time we are having and keep you
posted on how helpful I'm being. If you could
tell Mam and Dad that, that would be great.

CHAPTER 14

I must have fallen asleep after all. The sun is piercing the canopy above our heads. The beams of white light are brighter and shine all around us. My long, knotted hair is spilling all over the floor of the boat and I can feel drool dribbling down the side of my face. I fell asleep and did that once in maths, and my teacher, Mrs Holder, went crackers. I would have got away with it, but the drool made my exercise book stick to my cheek. Here, though, in the Amazonian jungle, our boat wedged into a muddy banking with giant trees towering overhead, it's broken leaves and bark that I have to brush away from my face.

The whistling sounds have gone – but so has Juan.

'Juaaan!' I holler, as loud as my sleepy throat will allow. 'Juaaaaannnnn! Where are you?'

My bum is sore. I don't know how I managed to drift off – this thing isn't exactly comfy and I can definitely feel a flip-flop-shaped mark on the side of my face. A shallow layer of water in the bottom of the boat has been my mattress for the night, and shielded from the full glare of the morning sun by all these trees, there's no way of getting dry. I'm in the same T-shirt and shorts I was wearing when Auntie Marg and I left the hotel two mornings ago. I give myself a sniff and, to be honest, I don't smell great. My hair's matted like a giant rat's tail too – I would love to see Mam try and get a brush through this. Don't laugh; I don't normally let her brush my hair or anything, but if we have a family party or something she likes to plait it and play with it. What is it with girls and hair?!

The bank next to me looks like it's covered in hair, with so many roots poking through the surface. It's pretty steep but it's totally climbable. The roots are good footholds, so if I throw myself at this one – brill! Landed it – with my trainer in the first knotted root, I can lever myself up to grab the next one with my right hand. One more pull and—

'Arghhh!' I cry.

A thud, a painful sting, and I'm on the banking, but I definitely didn't want to land on whatever it is that's sticking into the back of my left leg now.

'What the flipping heck is that?' I yell, twisting around to get a better look.

A huge red spear-shaped twig is sticking out of my inner thigh, a slow trickle of red blood creeping from the wound. It's burning, as if the twig is on fire.

In a second, Juan is standing over me. He puts one foot on my hip and, standing over me like a warrior over a slain victim, bends down and yanks the twig from my leg.

'Aaaarghhhh!' I scream again. 'That really hurt, you nutter. A little warning next time, please!' Tears are threatening the back of my throat and eyes.

'Come on, *llorona*!' Juan teases, shaking his head. He actually looks amused. He reaches into the boat, tears a long strip of material off a bag tucked under his seat and hands it to me. I snatch it from him, wrap it around my leg and tie a knot. I don't think I have done it right as it keeps slipping down my leg, but I daren't ask for help. Idiot. What kind of person yanks something out of your leg without even speaking?

Juan is already up on his feet and disappearing back into the undergrowth.

'Now where are you going?' I huff, following him and trying to keep the weight off my injured leg as much as I can. It's a good job I have stocky legs, otherwise I would be really pathetic. I'd have to get him to carry me, or something embarrassing.

Juan, five or six paces ahead of me, attempts a half-hearted wave, encouraging me to follow.

'Juan,' I try again, 'you said we were going back to the main river this morning.'

'Food and drink first,' he calls without turning around. He's pushing a pathway through the leaves and branches, and somehow he's timing it so by the time I reach them, they ping right back into my face, as if on elastic bands. It stings, but I'm not going to complain.

A few more paces and we reach a clearing. The leaves and branches have been pushed back to create a circle. In the middle there's a pile of bark, leaves and twigs. To one side, there's a heap of small wrinkled things that look a bit like old parsnips.

A pool of muddy water is off to the left. 'There's water over there,' Juan says, pointing in the direction of the swampy-looking pool.

'Oh. Right.' I gulp and head towards it. I *really* don't want to drink from that, but I don't want to act like a wuss. I start to bend down, cupping my hands, ready to scoop the murky liquid to my mouth.

'No!' Juan yells. 'Behind you!' He points frantically to just behind my head.

'What?' I spin round, confused.

'If you're going to drink from the ground, you dig a fresh hole *near* the pond – you never drink from an old, slimy pond like that one! But there's no need to do that either. It rained a few days ago, so we can drink whatever has collected on the leaves. Look!'

I turn and see that he's stretched a square plastic sheet between three trees, one corner tied to each tree with a plastic cord, and the fourth corner attached to a branch that's lower than the rest, just a metre from the ground. Water from the leaves above the sheet drips steadily onto it, and it's at an angle so that the water gathering there is running to one corner and dribbling into an empty plastic bottle – one of the ones I finished yesterday.

'The leaves are so large that they can collect a lot of rainwater. It usually falls straight to the ground, but if you can intercept it, you can drink it!' he explains. 'Like I told you, there are no shops here. There's no bottled water around. You could drink straight from the river or from that pond, but it would probably give you diarrhoea.'

Oh. I've only got one pair of clothes, so I really don't need *that* right now. 'Wow, Juan – that is pretty clever,' I admit, tipping up the bottle and swallowing some of the water. My mouth no longer feels like I've been chewing sand. 'Where did you get the plastic ties? How did you know how to do this? It's like something Bear Grylls would do!'

Juan smiles, busying himself with the pile of bark and leaves that he's collected by his feet. I pull out my phone and snap a photo of the water-collecting contraption. Even Gav has to be impressed with this. 'Did your dad teach you how to do it?' I continue. 'Or your mum?'

'Why all the questions about my family?' Juan

snaps out. 'It is not your business – I told you that already.'

I really need to stop doing that. He's so unbelievably touchy about his family – for whatever reason. 'Fine, sorry,' I mutter. 'Just wondering.'

Juan turns back to the little pile of parsnips he's crumbling. I walk over and peer at them, bending down next to him gingerly. The gash on my leg really stings.

'What is that?' I ask. 'Is it for a fire?'

He smiles. 'No. That's the other pile. This is poison.'

'What?!' I stare at him, and suddenly my heart's thumping again. Let's face it – I don't know this boy very well. Scratch that, I don't know him *at all.* How have I landed myself in this? I'm going to die in the jungle, I just know I am. 'Look,' I splutter, edging away from him. 'I know I shouted and I didn't mean to sound ungrateful and I know I threw your bag out of the boat, but I don't want to be poisoned, I don't—'

'For the fish, Amy,' he interrupts, scooping up a pile of the dark green crumbs into his hands. 'It's poison for the fish. Not for you.'

I'm confused and tired and my leg's so sore I can't concentrate. 'What? Why are we poisoning fish?'

'Amy, listen. We put this into the water, and the fish won't be able to breathe. They will rise to the surface, then we can catch them, cook them, and eat them,' he explains.

I thought you caught fish with a fishing rod or a net! The more time we spend here, away from Dudu, the more confident Juan seems – I don't think I've ever heard him speak so much before this morning.

'But . . . but if we eat the fish with the poison inside, won't we be poisoned too?' I ask uncertainly.

'No, trust me,' Juan says, nodding at the pile of green crumbs. 'Come on!'

I'm just going to smile and follow.

Gav, you're not going to believe it. You can catch fish by *poisoning* them! You grind up these funny-looking things, a bit like parsnips, sprinkle them in the water and wait a bit. At first nothing happens, then you can feel the fish tickling your toes as they go for the powder, and then, one after the other, they start to float to the surface. You don't need to catch them or spear them or anything. They come to you. It's ace!

You probably wouldn't be able to do it, though.

Amy
x

PS. I can teach you a brilliant trick when I get home, in case you ever run out of water on a camping trip or something like that. Actually scrap that, we don't live near a rainforest, and I don't think the Lake District gets enough rain for this to work. Oh well, I guess you've missed out!

CHAPTER 15

With an armful of fish, a satisfied look on his face and a plan to get the fire going, Juan is walking ahead, relaxed and confident.

'I'll be back in a minute. *Don't come after me,*' I instruct him, and he snorts. He knows what I'm talking about. The fact is, I need to wee. I've needed to for ages, but I didn't know where to go. I couldn't go in the boat, obviously, and I didn't want to hang over the side and wee into the river. I'm sure all those stories about the fish swimming up your stream of wee aren't true, but you never know. I suppose I could always keep stopping and starting, but I'd need to practise that.

I walk into the jungle until I can't hear or see Juan. My leg's still throbbing from my run-in with that killer plant, so it's hard to bend over, but I'm crouching as low as I can, squatting between giant waxy leaves.

It's dark when you look into the forest, as the tree trunks sort of grow around and over each other, and it's difficult to make one leaf out from another, or distinguish the darker shadows and dappled light on a tree trunk from a pair of—

Hang on.

'A pair of eyes?' I mutter quietly.

Quick – shorts up!

I'm low to the ground, level with whatever the pair of eyes belongs to, and I can hear it now: a clicking and chirping that I had thought was coming from a bird above me. It's small, with yellowy fur framing its face, tilting its head left then right as it tries to work out what I am. It's a little monkey, I realize with relief, and it's only a few steps away!

Slowly I reach for my phone and swipe it into camera mode. I click the button, and an image flashes on the screen briefly. The eyes are as bright in the picture as they are in real life. Sometimes at home I try and take photos of the kittens but they run, scared off by the flash. This little monkey, though, is going nowhere. Why isn't it scared of me?

Hesitantly I offer it my hand. It looks friendly, I think – I don't get the impression it wants to bite me, anyway. It pads forward, sniffs at my hands, then skips lightly onto my palm and up my arm, its warm, leathery feet tickling my skin and its fluffy tail flicking across my back.

'Juan! Juan!' I whisper, trying not to scare away the monkey. I creep in Juan's direction, the monkey perched on my shoulder.

Juan's back is turned, the pile in front of him starting to smoke. Out of the corner of my eye, I can see my new little friend lifting its head and looking at him.

Careful not to turn my body too quickly and knock it off its perch, I slowly turn my head to meet the little monkey eye to eye. Its nose is centimetres from mine. Its face is as black as coal, framed by white fluffy cheeks and thick hair on the top of its head.

'Look, Juan!' I call softly.

'What?' he says.

'I made a friend. This is . . . this is . . . *Eric*!' I

declare. 'He's friendly and cheeky. So he reminds me of my Grandad Eric. It fits!'

As Juan turns, the monkey leaps at him and Juan jumps backwards, clearly startled, and almost stumbles over the firewood he's gathered. The monkey, quick as lightning, bolts back to me, straight up my arm and onto my shoulder. It must like me! Again, I don't want to move too quickly – if the farm cats are anything to go by, wild animals don't like to be startled.

'What is it?' I ask Juan.

'A capuchin monkey,' he tells me. 'It cannot come in the boat with us, Amy.'

'But—'

Juan shakes his head firmly, pretending he wasn't scared or surprised.

He's skewered each fish on a long twig. I sit down by the fire, pick up a twig and begin to lower the fish onto the highest point of the pile and newest flame.

Juan shakes his head. 'Wait!' he says, putting his good hand on my arm.

'Well, are we going to cook them or aren't we?' I ask.

'Watch,' Juan tells me. Pulling me closer to him, he gently guides my hand and the fish to the lowest part of the fire where the twigs are glowing. Laying the fish down, it instantly sizzles. It's staring straight at me, its back arching in the heat as if its head is straining towards me, its scales crisping, black soot gathering on its body.

I wonder if it can feel the heat? I wonder if it is actually dead, or if the poison we used just paralysed it? I hope it's dead – well, if it wasn't before, it definitely is now.

Eric hops from foot to foot beside me as we eat. I didn't think I liked fish – *pescado*, Juan calls it – if it wasn't deep-fried in delicious crispy batter with chips and vinegar. I'm not keen on eating things that still have eyes, too. Just watching this fish be cremated as it eyeballed me was bad enough, and I am not even a vegetarian. But it turns out that when you're this hungry, you don't care!

After we eat, it's time to stamp out the fire. 'Let me,' I offer, stamping my Converse onto the glowing branches. With a puff of chalky ash and two hard thuds to the ground, the flames are out. The stamping has loosened the scab on my leg and I can feel a little trickle of blood running down my thigh, but I don't want to be called a *bebe* again, so let's pretend that didn't happen!

Juan is impressed, I think. Full and content, we head back to the boat. Juan's pushing branches and leaves aside again, only this time he isn't letting them ping back and smack me in the face. This time he is holding them until I pass.

The clicks, groans and whimpers of the jungle get quieter as the leaves begin to thin out and I can see the water again. It's like looking through a window onto a watery garden. Out there, beyond the leaves and branches, the water is racing by, a dark conveyor belt transporting huge branches and giant lily pads.

We climb into the boat. Lifting one leg up and out of the boat like a slow-motion karate kick, Juan places a foot on the banking and pushes us away. Slowly our boat begins to move, tearing a path through the water, and the gap between us and the banking starts to increase.

The highest, loudest, most indignant squeal

imaginable stops me in my tracks. I sit bolt upright as Juan bursts into laughter and points back at the riverbank. Our little friend is watching us leave and hopping up and down.

'He wants to come with us!' Juan explains.

I grin. I've never seen Juan laugh before. 'Well, come on then!' I shout before Juan turns grumpy again. '*Here!*'

I grab the paddle from Juan and lean towards the muddy shore, willing Eric to walk across it and board our boat. Only when the paddle is firmly touching the ground and I am leaning dangerously over the side of the boat does Eric skip down the splintered wood and hop in. Juan shakes his head, but he's still smiling.

'Let's go!' I say.

TOP TRUMPS

CAPUCHIN MONKEY

Highly intelligent monkeys who tend to live in the treetops in small groups.

Appearance:

Small, weighing only around 1kg when fully grown. (That's about the same as a little digital camera.) Capuchins have dark arms, legs and tails. The rest of their body is white or cream.

Top strength:

Very clever. They use stones to crush fruit so they can get to the nut. They have also learned to take the tips off some fruit so they can drink the juice inside. Some eat crabs, using stones and rocks to break the shells.

Most likely to be found:

In Central and South America, in the treetops during the day. They generally don't come out at night, as they hide from nocturnal predators.

Deadly?

Can be aggressive within their own group if fighting for the role of the most dominant male. Territorial – capuchins heavily urinate over an area to mark their territory.

SCARE RATING: 30 • DANGER RATING: 51 • COOL RATING: 92

TOP TRUMPS

CANDIRU FISH

Known as the vampire fish or toothpick fish, the candiru is legendary among Amazonian tourists. They feast on bigger fish by swimming inside them and then launching umbrella-like spines as anchors. Stories suggest the candiru can occasionally attack humans too, and many visitors to the Amazon cross their legs when they hear about the man who went to the toilet in the river and needed surgery, because the candiru swam up his stream of urine and locked onto his insides with its spiky spines.

Appearance:

Called the 'toothpick fish' because it is so small and slender. Its tail is slimy and hard to keep hold of, should it attack you. It is also translucent and therefore difficult to see.

Top strength:

Moves at lightning speed once they have identified a target (known as the 'host fish') and can wiggle their way into position within seconds.

Most likely to be found:

Lurking at the bottom of the river where it is dark and difficult for most other fish to see.

Deadly?

To other fish, certainly. Once the candiru has fed and exited its target, the fish is unlikely to survive. Its insides have been eaten, after all! They are unlikely to kill a human, although the person in question will need painful (and embarrassing) surgery.

SCARE RATING: 64 • DANGER RATING: 71 • COOL RATING: 63

CHAPTER 16

'My name is *Amy*,' I say loudly, hoping our little friend understands. He clucks and clicks like he is trying to answer. 'Your name is *Eric*,' I tell him.

We set off with Eric perched on the edge of the boat, his tail dangling over the side and resting against the words *Anna Maria*. He looks so cute that I take a picture. Then I press the little icon on my screen to flip the camera around, so that I'm looking at my own face. Time for a selfie.

I rub my teeth with the tip of my finger. Oh, yuck, they feel horrible – furry and like they have a coating of something sticky on them. My tongue is just as bad, and my hair is gross. Rebecca and Harpreet would be so embarrassed if they could see me now! Ha – I REALLY don't care about my hair here. It's not like I'm trying to impress Juan. My breath must stink too, like Mr O'Donnell, our history teacher. His breath is so bad that if you inhale when he's talking to you, it could kill you.

Mam is always sending me back into the bathroom to brush my teeth properly, so I don't usually have stinky breath. I moan at her, but I don't mind really. I don't want to smell. No one talks to the girls that smell. No one speaks to sweaty Sandra. Well, I do if no one is looking, but I don't want to be put in her sweaty outcast gang by my friends. Come to think of it – yep, a quick whiff of my armpit and I smell even worse than Sandra right now. I don't think I've ever wanted to brush my teeth or have a wash so much.

Eric won't mind, I'm sure. Smiling with my mouth closed so that my teeth don't show, I lean forward so that my face is next to Eric's and snap the selfie. Gav will be *so* jealous.

For the first time since we arrived here, the sky looks dark. Dark for the middle of the day, I mean. Thunderous almost, and there's an odd smell. It's a bit like mushrooms, a bit like damp bark.

'It's going to rain,' Juan explains, reading my

puzzled face. He stops paddling, and even Eric stares ahead as the clouds get thicker and faster. Suddenly everything is silent and still except for the sky.

'*Storm!*' yells Juan excitedly, standing up in the boat to meet it.

Within seconds I hear what he is waiting for: the noisy flush of a tap being turned on. That's what it sounds like, but it's actually the rain starting. It's coming our way and Juan looks excited.

I reach for my phone and slide it into camera mode. Swinging from left to right, I take an awesome panoramic shot: jungle, river, jungle, with huge grey angry clouds hovering above like a wave poised to crash down on us. Then I push it quickly back into its waterproof pouch before the rain starts.

First a drop on my head, then my arm, my leg. I stand up like Juan and brace myself for the rain, feet wide apart, shoulders back, head high, arms by my side. Two drops become four, and a light patter against the boat becomes a loud drumming, and suddenly a flood of cool water crashes down on us.

We stand one behind the other in our boat, Eric crouching, shivering, beneath my legs, his hands over his head. 'Quick! The bottles!' shouts Juan, tipping over everything he can find in the bottom of the boat until he lays his hands on the empty water bottles. He stands them upright in the boat, wedging them in place with his feet. '*Drink!* While you can!' he shouts as a flash of lightning illuminates the sky and the grey river looks white for an instant. A thunderclap echoes over our heads and Juan tips his head back and opens his mouth wide to catch the water.

I do the same. '*Wow* – this is amazing!' I yell through mouthfuls. Cold water streams over my face and through my hair. It feels like buckets and buckets of rain are being tipped over my head, and after days of being hot, sweaty, dusty and dry, it feels brilliant.

'We're being pushed back!' Juan shouts, screwing lids onto bottles full of rainwater. 'Let's head to the side. We can shelter until this passes.'

I stick one thumb up but I don't close my mouth or dip my head to acknowledge him   I don't want this to end!

Juan uses the oar to push us to the river's muddy edge, steering us underneath the overreaching canopy of leaves, so we're out of the rain. We both hang onto tree roots so that our little boat doesn't get pushed back upstream. The wind and the rain are so strong.

'It won't last long!' calls Juan. He's grinning, still buzzing from his unexpected shower. I've never seen him smile so widely.

'I feel *amazing*!' I squeal.

We listen to the rain, the thunder and the cracks of lightning. I scoop a soggy Eric into my arms and cuddle him to warm us both up, and Juan sees me and laughs, pointing to the sky again. Flecks of blue are creeping into sight and the sun is starting to break through the clouds already.

'That was the quickest storm ever,' I say. The drops of rain splashing into the river beside me are shrinking from the size of fifty pence pieces to peas in seconds. In just a couple of minutes it's all over, and we're getting ready to set off again.

Eric settles down on my lap and falls asleep almost straight away. I decide I'm going to take advantage of Juan's slightly more friendly mood. It might never happen again.

'Juan,' I say lightly, 'where do your family live? Will we get there today? I mean, how much longer are we going to be travelling? That storm was amazing; I loved it – but really, I don't think we should go too much further. My leg hurts and I think it needs looking at.'

I'm not just saying this – my leg is swollen up around the cut, and throbbing quite painfully. Mam would have smothered it in antiseptic cream by now – she goes through buckets of that stuff on me. I really did love that storm, and I don't actually mind the idea of sleeping in a boat again, but I'm not sure I want to sleep under these trees for another night. Not with whatever it is living in the top of them.

I'm not mentioning those sounds to Juan again, though.

'We should get there today, I hope,' Juan tells me. 'We are moving slowly because we have no petrol, and we have had to snake through the jungle. We can't take the most direct route – we don't want to be seen.'

'Why not? Are you trying to surprise them, or something?' I ask innocently. 'Hey, Juan, you're not trying to put off them meeting me, are you? Do you think your family won't like me? Look, I will be on my best behaviour, I promise. I might even need them to adopt me. After all, my mam and dad are probably going to disown me if Auntie Marg has rung them to tell them what happened. And that's probably the best scenario I can hope for. The other possibility is that Auntie Marg is so injured she can't even make a phone call!'

I try to inject a giggle into my voice, desperately hanging onto the possibility that Auntie Marg might be OK, sitting drinking a cocktail somewhere, and rolling her eyes at how dramatic I'm being. The truth is, I don't think she is. Her screams, the look on Dudu's face: she was hurt. I mean, really hurt, and it was my fault. I know now I shouldn't have run off. I know I should have stayed to see if she was OK, but I panicked and everyone was looking at me and I knew I would cry and when I cried at school in front of everyone Sally Anne tormented me for months. I thought if I hid for a day or so, Dudu would calm down and I could go and apologize and Auntie Marg would defend me, like she always does. 'Oh, she's just full of energy, our Amy,' she'd say. Only I didn't expect this to happen. Why do complications always happen to me?

Still, if Auntie Marg was here, she'd say, 'Embrace

it.' If Dad was here, he'd say, 'Toughen up, buttercup.' And I'll have to now. Miles along the Amazon, with nothing but groaning forest around me and miles of water ahead, I think 'Embrace it' and 'Toughen up' is perfect advice.

'No, I'm not trying to surprise my family,' Juan answers, interrupting my thoughts. 'I don't want to be seen by – by other people.' He shifts awkwardly in his seat. 'It is important that no one knows I am in this area.'

'Juan, what is going on?' I ask, unable to hide my suspicions.

Juan shakes his head. 'Forget it.'

Wow, he's SO annoying. One minute he won't tell me anything; the next, he tells me *just* enough to make me really curious and interested. Then he's back to saying nothing again.

'Juan, I just want to know what we're heading towards.' I try to speak calmly. 'Can't you just tell me . . . I don't know . . . if you've got any brothers and sisters?'

There are a few seconds of silence before he answers: 'I have a sister.'

He always looks so serious when I ask about his family. Part of me knows I shouldn't carry on, because he clearly doesn't want to talk about it, but I'm intrigued. I've never been able to control my mouth. It says what it wants, even when my brain is screaming at me to SHUT UP, AMY! 'What's her name?' I ask.

'Eva.'

'That's pretty,' I say.

'I have an aunt too, like you,' Juan offers. 'Tía Antonia. You will meet my sister and my aunt when we arrive.'

'And what about your mam? Will I get to meet her too?'

As soon as the words come out of my mouth I regret it. Juan's face goes tight, he stares straight ahead and clams up. 'Sorry,' I say. 'I didn't mean to—'

'We have to be there by nightfall,' Juan interrupts. 'That is when the caiman come out in this part of the river. So we need to hurry. We would have been there already – *if* we'd had petrol.'

His voice is cold. He was just starting to relax, and now I've ruined it! I wish I could go back in time and take my question back. I wonder why Juan got so upset when I mentioned his mam? I bet she and Dudu are divorced, like Kate's mam and dad.

'Juan, why don't you let me paddle for a bit?' I offer. I need to try and ease the tension. 'It's my fault that we don't have any petrol, so we're having to rely on the oar. Go on, let me have a go, and you can have a rest.'

Juan looks uncertain. 'I can do it! I'm not *totally* useless,' I insist. 'Move over, I've paddled loads of times before.'

Jumping to my feet, I take the oar from Juan. *You can do this*, I tell myself under my breath. *Every stroke is one closer to our destination.*

I *have* paddled loads of times before, but never in a boat like this – Gav and I often made a raft out of farm pallets and paddled it down the stream that runs behind the house. That means I have experience, right? There's just one paddle and I have to dunk it in one side, then quickly move it over to the other side, pushing us forward without sending us one way, then the other. Awkwardly I wrestle the oar, the clunky boat. Juan made this look easy . . . but I'm not telling him that.

Dear Gav,

It's fair to say this trip is taking me to places
I never expected to go! I'm being really
independent, just like Mam and Dad wanted.
Make sure you tell them that if you get this.
Anyway, you know when Dad lets us drive
the tractor in the fields and we're not meant
to? Well, I am driving a boat. In the Amazon.
It's not one of the biggest boats, but I am still
in charge. I'm moving people and animals up
and down the river to secret destinations. I
even have to keep it secret from you, because
we don't want the villages to be overrun with
tourists, so I can't tell you exactly where we're
going. All I can say is that it's pretty cool being
the captain of a boat on a secret mission.

Hope you're having fun with your friends. Doing
the same old thing with the same old people for
the millionth time.

Love
Amy
x

PS. Monkeys are so much better than cats.
They might even be as cool as dogs. Fact.

CHAPTER 17

The sun is high in the sky, burning so brightly it looks angry. If you told me right now I was on fire, I would believe you.

I *feel* like I'm on fire. Out in the boat, we're totally exposed. The creepy shadows and the sweaty moisture of the jungle are long gone, and in their place is a skin-blisteringly uncomfortable heat – it's like standing in front of the oven with the door open when Mam is cooking roast potatoes, and that must be about one million degrees, because the roast potatoes are so hot they spit and sizzle. Well, that's me now: I'm blistering and prickling and sizzling.

My hands look gross from gripping the paddle. The insides of my thumbs are white and puffy, the skin is already wearing thin, and my neck and my legs are aching. But I can't stop – it hurts to stop. As soon as I do, my muscles seem to realize what I'm doing to them, how hard I am working them, and they scream at me.

It hurts. *Everything* hurts. I feel a bit sick, too. At least moving the paddle from one side of the boat to the other brings a welcome splash of cold water. I lift the paddle high on purpose so droplets of water trickle down and hit me in the face.

To add insult to injury, while I sit here cursing and burning, Juan and Eric are acting as if they're on a cruise.

It was quite cute at first: the two of them sat up at the front of the boat, Juan waving when wash from the bigger boats came towards us, pointing and encouraging me in the right direction. Now the pair of them are lying back, Juan with his arms stretched behind his head, Eric resting his own little head on Juan's stomach.

'Oops, sorry!' I offer, as I accidentally on purpose smack the heavy wood against Juan's elbow. 'Sorry! I don't know why I keep doing that!'

Juan narrows his eyes at me. Then I see his gaze

flick to my red arms. At first I think he's going to laugh, but then he grabs his bag and starts rummaging around in it and I catch a glimpse of some little glass bottles – I think they're medicine – and a bag of rice. What use is that to us when we have no way to cook it? Idiot. I thought he was meant to know about this jungle living.

The remainder of the bag that was used to make the bandage for my leg is on the floor of the boat. Juan leans over the side, dips the cloth in the water, wrings it out and then wraps the fabric around my burning arms.

Straight away they feel better. 'Thanks,' I say, surprised.

He nods and points to the riverbank. 'Can you steer us closer that way?'

I wonder if this is a toilet stop, like when you pull in at the service station at the side of the motorway. But Juan's got his penknife out, and is crouched at the side of the boat. As we pull closer to the bank he reaches up and uses the knife to hack a huge, flat green leaf about the size of a golf umbrella away from a tree hanging over the water. Then he pulls some thick string from his bag and leans around me.

'What are you doing?' I ask, confused.

'Giving you some cover,' he grunts.

I turn around and realize he's strapping the leaf to the back of the boat, so that it curves right over my head like a huge, shady parasol.

'That's amazing,' I say. Sure, my arms are still in the sun, but my neck and back are suddenly in the leaf's cool shadow. It's a shame my ponytail's still soaked with sweat, heavy and sticking to everything.

Then I get an idea. 'Juan – can I borrow that knife?'

Juan stares at me.

'I'm not going to do anything stupid, you idiot!' I tell him, rolling my eyes. He passes it over and I rest the paddle in my lap, letting the boat float along by itself, hold the knife in one hand and grab my pony-tail in the other hand. Why haven't I thought of this before? Who needs long hair anyway?

I pull my hair away from my head, and rest the blade of the knife just above where the bobble sits. Juan eyes me, looking half uncertain, half amused. I take a deep breath – but I just can't get my hand to move.

'I need you to do it,' I tell Juan.

Juan's eyes widen. 'Me? No. No, I can't do it. If you change your mind—'

'I won't change my mind,' I tell him. 'I need it chopping off. It's driving me crazy. It's *so* hot. If I do change my mind I won't blame you, OK?'

Juan's muttering to himself. I catch the words '*Chica loca*,' whatever that means.

'Please, Juan,' I try. 'It's doing my head in and I'm so, so hot.'

'Fine.' Juan stands up, moves across the boat and takes the knife from me. 'Lean your head this way.'

My heart's thumping in my chest. I close my eyes, feel Juan grab my ponytail . . .

It only takes a moment.

'There.'

Everything feels lighter and cooler, all of a sudden. I stare at the handful of blonde hair that Juan's holding out to me, hardly able to believe what I've just done. I throw my hands up to my head. I can just picture my friends' faces now! They'd go mental if someone chopped off their hair! I laugh out loud at the thought of it.

My hands feel pretty much empty as I gather my remaining hair into a short ponytail. Once there was a waterfall of hair tumbling down my back, and now it's just a spiky stub.

'I like it. It's better,' Juan says.

'It *feels* better,' I agree. 'I'm glad there's no mirror, though.'

Juan smiles and flicks a strand of newly-cut hair out of my eyes. 'You could cut it even shorter,' he suggests. 'More like mine?'

'No way!' I pull away, laughing. 'That's enough of a haircut for this year, thanks!'

CHAPTER 18

With my streamlined hairdo and new shady parasol, we're making good ground. We've reached an especially busy bit of the river. The boats are enormous, carrying rows of lorries; others are packed with containers; but most have passengers on board. The decks are full of people, some leaning over the side, others rolling in and out of colourful hammocks.

'Why has it got so much busier here, Juan?' I ask as another huge boat sails past us. 'That last boat was carrying a whole football team!'

'It is busy here because this is the point where several tributaries meet,' Juan explains. 'It is like four or five roads coming together and meeting at one point. We don't need real roads, despite what *some* people think,' he adds, an edge creeping into his voice. 'We have always used the river to move people, cattle, food, goods, from town to town. It causes more problems, putting in real roads.'

'Problems for who?' I ask.

'For everyone.'

The river is vast, wide and choppy now. As the boats spit out streams of frothy angry water, causing wave after wave, we bounce and bob around. Once, I lose my balance and slip out of my seat, causing the scab on my leg to crack and bleed.

'Paddling's much harder when it's like this, isn't it?' I say, pushing against the paddle hard with my shoulder and wincing at the pain in my leg. It's not healing very well.

Juan frowns. 'You should give it back to me now, Amy.'

I shake my head. I can't just give up as soon as it gets tough! 'No, I'm fine, I'm fine.'

'No, really.' Juan stands and reaches out towards me. 'You are not strong enough.'

The cheek! 'I've been paddling for ages now and I think I'm doing a pretty good job!' I tell him. My muscles are throbbing and my shoulders ache, but there's no way I'll admit that to him now. Not strong enough! I'll show him.

We need to get to the other side of the river. But it's like crossing a motorway. All the boats heading towards Iquitos are on one side of the river, and those going away from it are on the other side, but somehow, we're heading right across the middle, straight into the path of the oncoming traffic.

I grit my teeth and paddle as hard as I can, but the suck and pull of the water as it's churned up by the big boats is too strong. Another wave is approaching now, even bigger than the last, the white foam crawling towards us. 'I can do it,' I insist when Juan starts to speak again. 'I *can!*'

'No, you cannot.' Juan leans across, grabs one end of the paddle and starts to pull it away from me.

'Let go!' I cry, pulling it back.

We tug at separate ends – then a wave hits us, and knocks us both off balance. The paddle flics out of our hands and lands in the water, disappearing beneath the surface.

Our boat bounces to the left, then the right. 'Juan, that was *so* your fault—' I begin hotly.

But I stop when I see his face. His eyes are wide, gazing at something behind me. His mouth opens in horror. 'We have to jump. Now. Before it hits us,' Juan croaks, his voice hoarse.

'What?'

I look round. A huge red metal diamond dominates the sky behind me. I'd been so busy looking ahead, I hadn't noticed the ferry behind us. We've driven straight into its path – and with no paddle, and nothing else to steer us, we now have no control over where our boat is going!

The shadow of the ferry falls across our boat. *Hoooooooonkkkkkk!*

'They will not move for us! They can't, they are too close!' Juan yells, grabbing my arm.

This is it! I scoop Eric up and pop him on my shoulders, and his leathery little hands lock around my neck as I rest one foot on the side of the boat, take a deep breath and catapult my body up and over the side.

A second in the air, and then – *smack* – the water swallows my body. I kick for air as leaves, branches and what I hope are fish brush my legs. Eric is gripping my neck, his feet pushing against my ears muffling the honk of the boat as it thunders past, sucking me towards it, then pushing away. There's river water in my eyes and mouth. My clothes are heavy, my trainers are like lead.

Luckily I'm good at swimming: I really am – I have to be, as Gavin only lets me play in the stream at the bottom of our house with him and his mates if I can keep up. He'd be good at this – he can swim across that stream and back faster than anyone I know.

Rocks are scratching my knees, so I must be at the edge. My hands claw through knotted roots underneath my feet. 'Juan?!' I splutter as Eric skips from my head to the shore. He looks smaller and skinnier than he did five minutes ago, and he's shaking his head from side to side, his fluffy yellow cheeks dripping.

I pull myself out of the water. Looking back, I can see our boat already splintered into dozens of pieces, the river throwing up bits of wood and the plastic buckets we had on board.

Juan has pulled himself out of the water too. He's

watching the boat disappear downstream, piece by piece. His arms hang by his side. His head is bowed, as if Dudu were here, shouting at him.

He looks broken, like his boat.

Dear Gav,

You know I don't really cry, especially not to you, but sometimes you just need a good cry and this is one of those times. You can't judge me or torment me because you have NO idea what it's like here. It's not a holiday. I can't believe you thought this was a treat. It's been HARD work. In real life, this jungle – well, it's a bit more creepy than even the telly made out. You need to keep your wits about you.

I haven't been totally honest with you. The truth is – and I can confess this because I'm pretty sure I won't ever actually be brave enough to send you this email once I'm somewhere that has wifi – the truth is that Auntie Marg, she's not well. At all. I have no way of finding out exactly how not well she is, though. I ran away with Juan by accident, and now we're stuck in the jungle with no boat and no food and only each other.

Juan isn't a murderer or anything. When I hurt my leg, he helped me. But there's something not right about him; whenever I try and talk to him or ask him stuff he loses his temper and snaps. Mam always tells me to think before I speak and I am trying! I just always put my foot in it. Juan won't even tell me exactly where we're going. Not that we can go there, now that we have no boat!

Anyway, if you EVER get this email, just remember that this is no holiday.

Amy
x

CHAPTER 19

'Could we build a new boat?' I ask.

Juan's back is still turned, his arms still folded. He's been like that for ages: silently seething. At first he was shouting stuff in angry Spanish, and the way he looked at me confirmed what I already knew. This is my fault.

Ashamed and frustrated, with tears still burning the back of my eyes, I know I can't get upset. It will only make things worse. I need to be positive, I need to try and come up with a solution – right?

'Could we flag down one of the big boats to pick us up? Like a bus? There are loads of people on them already, so surely they wouldn't mind a couple more?' I suggest cheerily, painting a fake smile on my face.

'Don't be stupid! They stop at towns – they don't

stop just anywhere,' Juan spits. His eyes are red and his face angry, like Dudu's. 'Besides, it's too shallow for them to stop here.'

'OK, OK. Well, is there a town nearby? One we could walk to?' I ask cautiously. I nip my arm to stop myself from crying again. Now is not the time to be a baby, I tell myself.

Juan shakes his head and starts to walk away from me, further into the jungle.

I suppose we travelled from sunrise to sunset yesterday, and most of today – even though that was just paddling – so we must have come pretty far. The houses we have seen have been few and far between. Each one sat on stilts, and all were made of some sort of pale wood. Pretty, but they weren't *towns*.

'Even if we *were* in a town, we couldn't pay for a lift, since we don't have any money. My bag, with the rice and medicine and all the other things I was taking to my family, is floating down the river,' Juan shouts over his shoulder in my direction.

Oh, now I feel *really* bad.

I forgot about the stuff in that bag, and I'm not going to say it to Juan, I'm not, but I'm guessing that's part of the reason for this visit. To take things to his family. I sigh heavily. Never mind tears; now my head is filled with guilt and regret. What do I say? I rack my brain.

'If something goes wrong in our house, my mam says, "You have to laugh, otherwise you'd cry!" It works, Juan! Because, you know, what other option do we have? We can't sit here crying for ever, can we?' I say, hoping this might snap him from his mood.

'Amy, be quiet!' He turns and stares at me. 'We have no food. Thanks to you. No boat. Thanks to you. No water, thanks to you. We have nothing. We are still half a day from where we need to be. You see what happens when you don't listen! From now on, do as I say – or I will leave you behind!'

Brilliant. Said the wrong thing. AGAIN!

I still have my phone, in its ugly waterproof pouch, and it looks like it's still working. My Top Trumps cards are tucked in there too. I won't mention that to Juan, though – he probably wouldn't appreciate it.

'Amy!' he barks from up ahead.

'*Coming!*' I yell, stomping after him.

'We need to swim the rest of the way. There is

a freshwater stream near my family home and I'm sure one of its tributaries runs through this part of jungle. Obviously we would be unable to swim in the main river itself – those strong currents would sweep us to our death – but it is possible to swim down a tributary like this. If we follow it, it should take us to where we need to be.' He glares at me. 'You can swim, can't you?'

'I swim all the time at home – yes, I can swim, of course I can swim,' I say, trying to be positive, 'but I'm not entirely sure I want to get back in this river. Those fish . . . if they can swim up your wee, can they swim into an open cut? I think I could stick my finger into the hole in my leg left by that spiky twig . . . It's still bleeding. And what about Eric?'

Shaking his head, Juan wades into the jungle, effortlessly stepping over branches and leaves that almost come up to his waist. I try to copy him, but I'm much more awkward. Knotted vines pull at my feet and slow me down, branches smack me in the face and leaves tangle in my hair.

'Juan! I have to stop for a minute. I'm having a sit-down!' I yell into the shadows ahead. I can't actually see him any more, but I can hear crunching and cracking as he cuts his way through the dense jungle. I perch on a mossy, moist-feeling log, and Eric, who's been skipping effortlessly from branch to branch, settles next to me. 'We'll be OK, won't we, Eric?' I ask, stroking his furry head, looking for reassurance.

Juan's head appears in a gap in the waxy leaves. I think he's going to tell me to get a move on, but instead he throws me something. An orange.

'I *love* oranges!' I say, digging my fingers straight into the peel.

'Don't sit there for too long,' Juan warns me, nodding at the log as he peels his own orange. 'It's the perfect place for spiders.'

'I know you're just saying that to scare me, Juan, but I actually *love* spiders,' I tell him, throwing my orange peel at him. The pieces are sweet and juicy and make my mouth tingle, they're so delicious.

'The jungle beyond this point is so thick with trees and roots that swimming is the fastest way,' he explains as we eat. 'We will have to be quick. We shouldn't be here when it is dark.'

'Why, what happens when it's dark?' I ask.

'You can't see where you are swimming.' I can hear the exasperation in Juan's voice.

'Oh. Right. Sorry, obviously.'

'And the caiman come out,' he adds. 'And the capybara.'

'The what?'

'Capybara. A bit like rats. There could be snakes too.' He nods towards Eric. 'The monkey will have to sit on your head.'

So back in the water we go.

Right, I can't act all precious now. Juan is swimming ahead of me but he keeps looking back, presumably to see where I am. He keeps diving underneath the surface and dipping out of sight, and soon it's mostly only his head I can see bobbing along. Every now and again his right hand breaks the surface, then the left leg, then maybe the left hand. He's got no order or real technique to his swimming, but he's moving quickly.

'Will you slow down, please?' I call after him, but either he doesn't hear me, or he's ignoring me.

I'm usually quicker than this, but my leg has started

to feel numb. The throbbing pain is fading, but it's been replaced by a tight, tingling feeling, right down to my toes. If Gavin was here now I would do to him exactly what I am about to do to Juan. If I give a couple of really strong kicks and reach out, I can just about . . . yep . . . *got him*. I've grabbed his ankle and if I give it one massive pull . . . yep, he's gone under. His head has totally disappeared and I can swim over the top of him if I breaststroke quickly. I surge forward with one massive pull, and just as I see his thick black hair break the surface as he comes back up for air, I dunk him straight back under.

It's OK, I won't hold him down there for too long – I don't want him to drown or anything stupid! In a matter of seconds he's back at the surface, coughing and spluttering. 'Why did you do that?!' he gasps, spitting river water with every word.

'You were racing ahead! Showing off! I don't know where I'm going, remember? Eric and I could get lost in here! And what about all those creepy things your dad was telling me about? Pink dolphins, piranha, caiman— Arghhh!' Something touches my leg and suddenly I can't breathe.

'The faster we move, the less likely we are to run into them,' Juan says, and I sense he's losing patience. 'You have to keep up. Come on.'

Before he can set off again I throw myself backwards into the water, legs straight like I'm wearing skis, arms whizzing up and over my head without interruption. 'Come on, slowcoach,' I shout over the splashes.

Normally when I'm doing backstroke at the swimming pool in town I follow the ceiling tiles, using them as a guide to keep me in a straight line. Otherwise I end up ploughing straight into the person next to me and smacking them in the face. I don't mean to do it, obviously. Once, I smacked a girl so hard that her lip burst. There was blood everywhere and we all had to get out of the pool. She was hamming it up, only crying because some little kid next to her started to be sick at the sight of the blood. It was all a bit over-dramatic.

There are certainly no handy ceiling tiles here. There is a funny pattern, though, of leaves and branches, some stretching way above my head, others only metres above me. On the ones closest to me, I can make out veins and patterns running through the leaves. Just above them is—

'Juan! What's that?'

Juan looks up to where I'm pointing. Clinging to a tree trunk is a greeny-grey furry pile, a head tucked under a body. It's not moving, not even to look and see what the noise below it is.

'It must be a sloth!' I realize, even before Juan has managed to answer me. I read about them in my pack of Top Trumps cards. They hardly move at all, and when they do, they only slide forward a few centimetres at a time. Their eyes are really far apart too, which means they look a bit confused. They sound kind of boring – they sleep all day.

There's a ripple from behind me, a splash, and—

'Ouch!' Juan's foot scoops my legs from under me, and at the same moment his hand pushes my shoulder, and I'm under – my face down into the water, a mouth full of wet leaves to go with it.

One–all, I suppose.

SLOTH

There are two types of sloth: two-toed and three-toed. Both types are cute, move very slowly, and are difficult to spot.

Appearance:

They look a bit like out-of-shape monkeys with browny-grey fur, that can appear green because they move so slowly that algae actually grows on them. Sloths often curl up in a ball to sleep, tucking their head between their arms so they blend in with the tree. Their heads are flat and their bodies are roughly the same size as a small dog. They have hook-like claws used for hanging onto trees.

Top strength:

Can sleep and even give birth upside down. Excellent at camouflage and good swimmers!

Most likely to be found:

Sloths generally stay in one tree for at least a couple of days at a time, and have been known to live in the same tree for years. They don't need a lot of food, munching on fruit, young twigs and leaves.

Deadly?

Not unless you die of boredom, watching them!

SCARE RATING: 19 • DANGER RATING: 21 • COOL RATING: 52

CHAPTER 20

'How much further?' I yell, trying to prevent my mouth from dipping beneath the surface of the muddy water.

'Not far!' Juan answers, spinning on his back to speak to me.

The sun is starting to set, and just like last night, that mysterious shrieking and calling noise is filling the canopy above our heads. My legs feel like lead, my fingers are pruned, my arms sore and my shoulders are burning. I don't want to complain, I don't want Juan to think I'm being a baby. My clothes are heavy and my Converse trainers – well, I would have kicked them off ages ago as they're so weighed down with water but Juan shouted at me not to.

'There are fish around here that will pierce right

through your feet,' he warned. 'Their bones are so sharp that if you stand on one, the bone can go right through and come out the other side.'

'Thanks for telling me that *before* I got in the water,' I huffed, and Juan replied, 'Don't worry. There are not as many of those fish as there are caiman.'

It's funny – I've *almost* stopped caring about the things that might injure us. Or eat us. Or drown us. All I can think about is how much I hurt.

All I want to do is stop swimming.

I spot something on the other side of the river. I blink and squint against the setting sun, and I think I can see . . . a woman. 'Hey!' I yell to her. 'Look, Juan, look over there!'

I blink again and try to focus. She has thick long dark hair like a pop star's – just like one of the girls in Little Mix – spilling over her shoulders and down to her waist, just like mine used to. She looks like a doll, a gorgeous doll. I start to kick my way towards her. I need a rest, just a little rest, and maybe she has some food. And clean clothes, these clothes feel so horrible.

I think she's smiling, and it makes me smile. It's so

nicc to see a smile after Juan's teasing and tormenting, his huffs and grumpiness. My legs are kicking more slowly now, but I don't care. I'll just have a little rest and . . .

'*Amy!* Where are you going? We're nearly there. *Don't* stop now!' calls Juan.

'I'm just going to take a quick rest with that lady over—' I scan the shoreline to point her out to Juan – but she's gone! Her glorious smile, her beautiful hair: all gone. The bank is empty in the evening sun.

'Come on, Amy!' Juan barks.

The moon is creeping into the sky. Eric swings and leaps through the tree branches above us; he perched on my head for about five minutes earlier before deciding he'd had enough of that, so now he's making his own way, occasionally stopping to peer down at us. I've almost lost sight of him now that the light is fading. 'I thought you said we shouldn't swim in the dark?' I call. 'Should we get out and walk the rest of the way?'

'We're nearly there!' Juan replies, shouting over his shoulder, then disappearing under the surface again.

Why does he keep doing that? I daren't – I'd

probably swallow something horrible. I can't decide if he's brave or stupid for swimming underwater. I keep remembering the candiru fish, the ones that are meant to swim up people's streams of wee. If they can do that, surely they can also swim inside your mouth and down your throat? What happens then? Do they go in your tummy and eat what they find inside you? If one did go in my belly, it would have to burrow its way out through the skin to get back to its mates – that would be sure to hurt. A lot. So for now I'll keep my mouth tightly closed whilst swimming, and I certainly won't wee. Just in case . . .

'There it is!' shouts Juan, nodding ahead.

The pace of his swimming picks up. He's getting closer to the riverbank and I realize he's heading for a wooden jetty stretching over the water, silhouetted against the night sky.

For the first time all day I don't want to catch up with him. I'll let him go first. Now that we're here I'm feeling nervous. Dudu seemed friendly at first, but as soon as the crash happened he turned pretty scary. What if all Juan's family are mean? What if Juan and Dudu left because they were all awful? I have aunties that we avoid – apart from at Christmas, when we *have* to see them. Maybe Juan doesn't talk about them because they're mean.

No – don't be stupid, my stupid tired brain. He's been desperate to get here, hasn't he?

Juan pulls himself out of the water and onto the wooden jetty, calling out in Spanish, and I follow slowly. Finally, after all these miles, I can see Juan's home.

It's the home he's mentioned, but barely described: a small wooden house on stilts, with ladders stretching to the long grass beneath it. There don't seem to be any outside walls, so I can see right inside; candles light up one room full of colourful hammocks, and another next to it which has a large wooden table in the middle. There are chickens everywhere, and lots of people spilling out of the house, all of them coming this way.

It's too dark to see if they're boys or girls, but most of the crowd are tall and skinny, like Juan. Juan rushes forward to meet them, and noisy, loud, confusing Spanish chatter fills the air.

'*Bienvenido a casa, Juan!*'

'*Juan! Ha vuelto!*'

People are talking over each other, and some are attempting to hug Juan, but he's brushing them off. Such a boy.

I hang back, and hear Juan mention my name. I smile awkwardly as faces turn towards me curiously. 'Er, hi,' I say, waving. I'm dripping wet and doing my best not to shiver. If Mam was here she'd go over and start talking – she'll talk to anyone – but it's hard when you don't know the language.

One of the tallest men is coming my way. Oh no – what's he going to say? I can't remember how to say 'my name is' in Spanish – hours in the water have numbed my brain.

But the man pushes past me, his eyes on the river, his arm outstretched, pointing towards the dark water where I was swimming just a few minutes ago. Some of the men and lots of the kids are following him, swallowing me into their group as they lean over the jetty and point. Elbowing my way through the crowd of strangers, I look down.

The moonlight bounces off something floating through the water. A rock? A log? It's about the length of three cricket bats laid end to end, with three bumps along it. I can't work out what it is until a pair of glinting eyes blink and a strong jaw lined with sharp teeth snaps – then I realize that the bumps are a head, a body and a long, flat tail.

A cold feeling creeps into my bones as I realize this thing was following me and Juan. It was just minutes behind us, following us for who knows how long.

A caiman.

SIREN

Mythical women, so beautiful men cannot stop staring at them. They are believed to encourage men to enter the water and attempt to swim across the river. Few men are strong enough to survive the currents and stare so intently with their eyes and mouths wide open that they often drown in the mighty Amazon river.

Appearance:

Stunningly attractive women, but there is no definitive description as everyone sees different things. They usually have long hair, lean bodies and a piercing smile.

Top strength:

Disappear as fast as they appear. No one can get to them quickly enough to talk to them or see if they are real.

Most likely to be found:

By the water's edge, opposite the factories where loggers chop and prepare wood. Anywhere near a work force: Brazil nut-farmers, men searching for gold or those who farm rubber from trees.

Deadly?

Most certainly. Many men have disappeared completely in the rainforest.

SCARE RATING: 32 • DANGER RATING: 73 • COOL RATING: 74

CAIMAN

The largest predator in the Amazon.

Appearance:

Much like a crocodile but with a narrower body and slightly longer tail. They can be brown, green and even grey with scaly skin. Their large heavy heads are good for catching prey. Black caiman are the biggest of six species of caiman found in the Amazon, growing over 6 metres long.

Top strength:

They are so ferocious few dare attack them. Jaguars and humans are the caiman's only real threat. Some weigh up to 500kg. Caiman can also swim at speeds of up to 30 miles per hour.

Most likely to be found:

Tend to live alone in slow-moving water and marshy swampy areas; they are nocturnal so you will see them only at night.

Deadly?

Definitely. Any member of the alligator family is predatory, and black caiman are among the most feared predators in the world.

SCARE RATING: 94 • DANGER RATING: 99 • COOL RATING: 91

CHAPTER 21

A little kid with wide eyes and a mop of dark hair grabs my hand and drags me towards the crowd. 'Hello,' I say awkwardly, digging my feet into the ground and trying to slow the pace at which I am being dragged. 'I mean, er, *hola!*'

Now that I can make out individual faces, I can see they look happy. Thank goodness they seem glad to see Juan. Everyone is patting and hugging him, and now it's my turn for inspection. Within seconds I'm in the middle of the group, and although they're still firing questions at Juan, they're looking at me.

The older ones seem suspicious: eyebrows high, brows creased. Juan's reassuring them, I think – I hope – as they pepper him with questions in exactly the same way Mam interrogates Gav about his muddy football kit.

No one is fully clothed. Most of the men have shorts on, but there aren't many T-shirts. Even the women are pretty much topless, opting to wear layers of colourful necklaces and beads rather than layers of fabric. I'm trying not to stare, but it's hard not to. Everyone is tanned with thick, dark hair. Some of the men have hair longer than the women!

One woman takes hold of my arms and is looking at me intensely, staring right into my eyes. Her eyebrows are bushy and thick and she looks old, but she has a strong grip. At least, I think she is old, because she is pretty wrinkly – she looks a bit like one of those dogs with the squashed-up faces, the really cute ones. Why is it OK for dogs to be wrinkly, but not humans? Mam is always putting her face cream on so she doesn't get wrinkles, but they look kind of cool on dogs. I tried to tell Mam that one day but I don't think she got what I meant.

Another woman wearing a skirt, but no top and no shoes, with long black hair falling to her waist and covering most of her chest, comes forward and smiles at me, and Juan says, 'This is my aunt, Antonia.'

The words are coming thick and fast. They are asking questions about me, but I can't understand what they are saying. They are all looking at me, looking me up and down, and within minutes the exploratory hands are dragging me towards the house, towards the golden candlelight illuminating rooms on stilts. The children have already wandered away – the one who dragged me to the group in the first place has long since disappeared – just the grown-ups are left. They are leading me to the house, which close up looks like a massive tree house, only not in the trees.

A familiar leather grip takes hold of my finger. 'Eric! You're here!' I squeal, delighted to see his familiar wrinkled little face, his friendly eyes, his fluffy cheeks almost glowing in the moonlight.

Inside the house, my wet, filthy, blood-stained shorts and T-shirt are peeled from my bruised and scratched body. 'Easy! Get off!' I protest, but they're taken away before I can snatch them back. Juan's aunties leave the little waterproof pouch around my neck with my phone and cards intact, though.

I like bruises, to be honest – I am generally quite proud of the ones I get at home – and here the ladies seem equally impressed, tapping the biggest ones on my shins and arms. I'm bending over to try and cover my exposed body. The aunt with the really long hair is passing me a clean T-shirt and shorts.

'Quick! Quick!' I shout, the realization that I am stark naked in a shed-like building with no doors hitting me like the breeze I have just felt on my skin. There are loads of boys! And Juan is wandering around somewhere!

I throw myself into the clean clothes, and it's really nice putting something dry and warm on. At home, when it's really cold in the winter, Mam puts our clothes on the Rayburn cooking range so they'll be warm when we get into them. She'd do that for me now, because I'm suddenly aware of how cold I am – Juan and I were in the water for hours and I swear I can feel the cold in my bones. Mam would sort that out, and she'd put a massive plaster on my leg, and we wouldn't mention it again because she knows I hate it when anyone makes a fuss. I hate the way these women are fussing. Mam knows me, and these women don't. My eyes are burning with the familiar threat of tears.

'Please stop touching me, it's fine,' I plead as the oldest woman pokes the cut on my thigh. 'Seriously, get off!' I protest, trying unsuccessfully to bat her hand away as she begins to unpeel Juan's home-made bandage. She might be skinny, but her grip is impressive – I can't move my leg. 'It will be fine if you *just* leave it!' I argue, wriggling as she starts squeezing the skin together, cracking the yellow scab and making it bleed again.

She takes a step back, sighs, slaps me on the arm in an oddly playful way, then walks out of the room muttering something in Spanish. I look at Eric, who's still by my side with a worried look on his face.

Juan's auntie has taken my wet Converse trainers, my naked toes clenching the knotted wooden floor. I can feel dust and tiny stones under my feet. They're covered in angry red bites I picked up in the river – from what, I don't know. No one else is wearing shoes either.

Just as I am pulling my shorts lower to cover the

cut on my leg, the old woman comes back in, her walk purposeful. Her hands are even faster now as she grabs my leg and smothers a thick red paste over my thigh and into the wound.

'Arghhhhh! That really hurts!' I shout, the paste burning my skin and tears pricking my eyes. I reach for my leg, desperate to claw the ointment off my skin, but the woman's lightning-quick hands halt my attempt. She nods and smiles encouragingly. Within a minute or so the paste cools. As my body relaxes, so does the old woman. She leaves the room, mild laughter rippling through her body.

There's only one person left in the room with me now: a girl who's a little bit older than me. Unlike the older women, her hair is bobbed. She points at herself, smiling. '*Me llamo Eva.*'

Eva. So this is Juan's sister!

'Hi, my name is Amy,' I reply. 'That's Eric. Or *Erriiiiique*, in your language.'

Eva nods, locks her fingers into mine and leads me through the rooms, towards the laughter and voices on the other side of the house. I'm not too sure I like her holding my hand – it's a perfectly nice hand, but

I don't really like holding hands. I like keeping my hands in my pockets. It feels a bit rude to pull away, though, and she's got such a nice friendly smile, and even friendlier eyes.

'Eric!' I call, even though I know he is right behind me, using him as an excuse to take my hand out of hers and put my arms out to him.

Through a spider's web of hammocks and along the porch, I follow Eva towards the voices. Occasionally heads poke out of hammocks and around corners, and pairs of eyes stare as Eva encourages me and Eric to follow her. Some of the tiny kids giggle and I smile back as widely as I can.

Finally we walk through a curtain of beads to find Juan in the middle of a group of men. Most are old – as old as Mam, Dad and Auntie Marg – although some are much older. I can see a resemblance between Juan and most of them, so they must be his uncles and cousins. They're all laughing and smiling, hanging on Juan's every word as he tells a story. I wonder what he's saying?

'*A ella le estaba dando un ataque!*'

His uncles seem to be finding it hilarious. They

laugh and ruffle his hair, like Auntie Marg does to me sometimes. Well, like she used to. The uncles keep calling Juan something, a sort of nickname. They say it and he sort of shrugs and smirks, half embarrassed, half proud. It sounds like 'Sackee', or— Hang on, I know what they're calling him. I've heard it before: *Saci pererê!* That was one of my Top Trumps cards!

I finally understand something they're saying! I want to join in the laughter, but they stop as soon as they see me enter the room. With everyone's eyes on me again, I pick my nails nervously. Normally, if everyone at school is looking at me, I can hide behind my hair, but what's left of it is slicked back, still wet from the river. I have nowhere to hide.

'Hiya!' I say, as brightly and boldly as I can with an over-enthusiastic wave. My heart's pounding in my chest.

Laughter. Thank goodness. Who knew? Looks like I'm funny in Peru!

Heads shaking and brown glass bottles being chinked, and one or two of the men mimicking my 'Hiya', the others turn back to Juan as he picks up the story. At one point I hear Dudu's name in the casserole of Spanish words. When he's mentioned, one man in grubby denim shorts without a top on taps Juan on the leg, another, one of the eldest in the group, pats his arm, and they both pull that face that grown-ups do when something sad has happened. You know, a sort of 'There there, everything will be OK' kind of face. No one seems to mention his scarred hand. It's not a new injury.

The women are less interested in Juan's story, occasionally turning and smiling at him, but generally busying around pots and pans in what must be the kitchen in this house. There's a shelf piled high with different coloured fruits and vegetables, but no fridge or washing machine.

One of the women hands me a bowl of hot brown stew. It looks gross, and I don't have a clue what it is, but I actually don't care – it could be guinea pig again, for all I know, but it smells amazing. I scoop it up with my hands and practically inhale two bowl-fuls. My tummy is full for the first time in days and I smile gratefully at the woman.

Eva places a bowl of purplish berries by my feet. I'm too full to touch them, which is a good job, as

Eric has buried his face in the fruit, guzzling away like he hasn't eaten in years.

The others are drinking some sort of milky yoghurt liquid. One of the women, a young, pretty lady with shiny hair wearing a T-shirt dress and massive earrings, is chewing and gurgling something in her mouth, then spitting it into the pan it's being served from. Whatever she's swilling around in her mouth is going straight into that pan, and Juan's uncles keep grabbing cupfuls of it. We get told off for spitting at home, but this family is actually drinking each other's spit. I thought I was seeing things at first, but it's definitely happening. Everyone seems to love it, though – there are smiles on everyone's faces.

'*Chicha?*' They offer me a cup. I sigh and pat my stomach, saying loudly and slowly, 'I'm full!'

No thanks! I can't get the noise out of my head: that throat gurgle you have to do to create enough spit. Eurghhh.

Juan has had three bowls of stew and two cups of the milky drink and he's still going strong. For someone that skinny, he can eat! I'm pretty sure two of the ladies – his aunt, and a much older lady with white hair – have been telling him off while he eats. His aunt is pointing at the pink, tender sunburn on my arms and the cut on my leg and whacking him on the arm playfully. It's hard not to giggle, especially as I think she's blaming him for my injuries.

The elderly lady keeps nodding her head at us and waving towards the room full of hammocks, where lots of Juan's little cousins and relatives are already sleeping – or *supposed* to be sleeping. '*A dormir,*' she barks. She's definitely urging us all to go to bed but I don't want to yet. I still don't know if they like me. I can't tell. Each person who passes, I try to catch their eye, nod and smile. Sometimes they smiled and nod back, though some of them seem wary, and a few of them have just ignored me.

'*Cuca!*' sniggers a small, chubby kid from his hammock while the old lady's back is turned. The room explodes into giggles. She spins around, scanning the hammocks, looking for the one who said it, her eyes narrowed, but there are too many kids in here for her to work out which one it was.

It must be some sort of cheeky insult . . . Wait. 'Cuca' – wasn't that on one of my cards? The word seems familiar. I pull the pack out of my plastic pouch and shuffle quickly through them. When I reach the one I'm looking for, I read it and grin. Juan throws me a questioning look, and I turn it his way so he can read it. He smiles.

I pull my phone out too and switch it on. There's no signal, not that I expected there to be one, so I still can't send any of the emails I've written to Gav – they're all still sitting in the 'drafts' folder – but I switch to camera mode and point it towards Juan.

He looks happy, his smile warm like the glow from the candles scattered all over the kitchen, and his body relaxed. He's wearing clean clothes and is working his way through a bowl of those purple berries. He sarcastically nods when his auntie tells him off, but they're both smiling, and it's playful.

It might be OK here after all, I think. It's not home, but it's not as bad as I first thought. The hammocks look inviting. I yawn and blink, and Eva nods towards an empty hammock in the next room, hanging close to the ground. I could definitely close my eyes for a few hours.

Eva effortlessly rolls me into the soft red hammock. There are no pillows, no blankets, and the gently-swaying material hugs me tightly, like only my dad can. Maybe I won't wriggle away from his cuddles so quickly in future. I'd love one now.

'*Buenas noches,*' Eva says softly.

By the time Eric scampers into the hammock and is curled up on my chest I'm almost asleep. His warm breath lands on my neck and the sound of him inhaling and exhaling mingles with the clicks and croaks of the jungle outside. My eyelids grow heavy. I close my eyes momentarily . . .

. . . and a rustling noise right underneath me sends them flying open.

I grab Eric, not allowing him to move, partly for his safety and partly for mine. I peek over the edge of the canvas. I lean closer to get a better look as several shiny black eyes lock onto mine. The creature freezes. I freeze. None of us can move.

The bluey-purple hairs on its legs are illuminated by light spilling into the room from the kitchen. It's smaller than a rabbit, but bigger than a hamster. It's a massive spider . . . about to have dinner!

CUCA

An old woman who punishes children who refuse to go to bed early.

Appearance:

Old, haggard and wrinkly. She has been described as a hag and a witch. Cuca hunches over a stick and shuffles rather than walks.

Top strength:

An evil stare so menacing young children may wet themselves if they meet her eye.

Most likely to be found:

Yelling at children playing in the early evening. Close to family homes and villages.

Deadly?

Believed to have evil powers but not considered deadly. She is certainly threatening, but there are no stories of her actually killing children.

PINK-TOE TARANTULA

Appearance:

Fully grown, they can be 15 cm long. Adults have black bodies with pink toes; youngsters have pink bodies with black toes. Most have a bluey-purple tinge to the hairs on their legs.

Top strength:

Can almost hypnotize victims by appearing to be in a trance-like state until they attack. They catch people off guard. In contrast, if they are attacked they are jumpy and skittish.

Most likely to be found:

In the trees, as the pink-toe likes to climb, and loves moisture and air. Some people believe that if pink-toe tarantulas live in groups they will start to eat each other, so they are most likely to be found living alone.

Deadly?

No. Not unless you want to scare your brother to death by leaving one under his pillow.

SCARE RATING: 94 • DANGER RATING: 51 • COOL RATING: 88

Dear Gav,

We are definitely going to have to have a word
with Mam when I get home. She needs to chill
out. I know she sometimes lets Bob sleep in
my bed, and from time to time Dad uses the
Rayburn in the kitchen to nurse poorly lambs,
but she still bangs on about hygiene when they
poo. Remember how mental she went when
she found a mouse in the hall? Here, no one
ever complains or gets stressed by animals.

Eric has already started sleeping in one of
the youngest kids' hammocks. Parakeets and
parrots, with outstretched green wings and red
heads, fly in and out of the kitchen. Sometimes
they pinch a berry, a nut or a seed. Other times
they perch for a second on a shelf or a chair,
but they fly off quickly again when someone
walks in. They're part of the family! There
are lizards and geckos, with their funny jerky
movements and sticky-out tongues. They dart
across the kitchen floor, moving from the shelter
of a cupboard to a corner, to a dark corridor,
only showing themselves for a few seconds
before they dart out of sight again.

Monkeys hang out in the kitchen, crawling all over the grown-ups and hanging from their hips like babies. One monkey even tried to drink milk from one of Juan's aunties, like new-born babies do! She batted it away, though! I would be so embarrassed if Eric did that – I feel kind of responsible for him!

Outside there are pigs and chickens, but not like at our farm – here they wander around completely freely. There are no fences, no paddocks, no sheds. All of this is watched over by a couple of huge birds that look a bit like storks crouched on the roof, bobbing and swaying as Juan's family wander about underneath.

I've taken loads of photos – you'll be amazed.

There is one creature in particular that I think you'd love the best. I'm going to bring you a very special souvenir home.

Love you. Sort of.

Amy
x

CHAPTER 22

'Eeeeouuuwww!'

Tap, tap, tap.

Creaaaakkkkk!

'Eeeeoooowww!'

Tap, tap, tap.

It's hard to tell what's close by, and even harder to work out what is making each noise, but I am growing to like them all. The high-pitched squeals, the echoing squawks; each morning the jungle's inhabitants pull me from my sleep. This is my third morning in the jungle and I'm getting used to the alarm call. The hammock, however, is much harder to master. Each day I crash out of the canvas, landing on the wooden floor in a tangle of arms and legs, and each morning Juan's cousins giggle.

I keep trying to speak to them, but they don't really understand me. They laugh when I try to join in and get stuff wrong, but it's not like Sally Anne laughs – this lot do it in a friendly way. Some of the adults still look at me a bit suspiciously, too.

Eva doesn't. Her smile is warm and reassuring. Without the approving nods from her, I would be out of here. Well, I probably wouldn't; I have nowhere to go. Juan and I will be going back to Iquitos soon, though, and when we get back, I'll go find Auntie Marg straight away.

Oh, Auntie Marg. Every time I think of her my stomach aches, like I've swallowed a bowling ball and my body is trying to digest it. That feeling hurts more than any of the scrapes I have picked up here.

In fact, pulling myself from the dusty floor and looking at my leg, I can see that the red paste which hardened on the first day and crisped on the second has almost gone. It's soaked into my skin, leaving an orange mark, but it's not nearly as sore and there's a thick dark scab over the cut. It's healing. I know a good scab when I see one.

I'm still wearing the shorts and T-shirt I was given

on day one. I don't have any PJs, but no one seems to.

As usual, it sounds like most of the family is up and about. I can hear lots of voices in the room next door, punctuated by the chopping of wood and the gentle clatter of pots on a stove. It's comforting, it sounds like home; even though this place is actually so different to *my* home, it still sounds like a family, starting their day. I smile, thinking of Mam and Dad, and Bob at my feet while we all sit at the breakfast table.

Juan's cousins brush their teeth in the kitchen with normal toothbrushes, but the older people use sticks and twigs, and instead of toothpaste they use a black chalky powder. I don't know what it is, but it tastes like cherries. It doesn't make your teeth black, though, and it's actually quite refreshing.

After a weird teeth-rub, I head into the bushes for a wee. Eva showed me the loo on my first night here: a shed on stilts, with a narrow plank to sit on. I'm not going there, no chance – everyone can hear what you're doing because there is no door. Only a worryingly stained curtain! No, I'm going to find myself a nice, private tree.

I walk out onto the wooden porch, jump down into the long grass, land awkwardly – luckily no one's around to see – and push past some low bushes into the jungle. As usual I don't have to look for very long: there's an enormous tree right ahead of me, with a funny bulging trunk, and roots that sit on the surface of the ground as high as a fence. It's amazing – the biggest tree I have ever seen. With those roots like fences, it's perfect. So private. Miles nicer than that stinky shed on stilts and I don't have to worry about anyone hearing me do a number two.

When I'm done I head back to the house and follow the sound of chattering children. Some of the littlest kids are naked, and gathered around a gecko, its bulging eyes blinking and twitching. They're laughing and giggling as they try to feed it. I take a photo of the gecko and a few of the kids. Behind them, Juan is counting slender arrows and shoving them into a cloth bag, points-up. His head is bowed and he's whispering something in Spanish to his uncle, who is staring at Juan and nodding, his arms folded.

'Juan, what's going on?' I interrupt.

Juan sees me watching and frowns. 'Nothing,'

he tells me. 'Just talking. It is not your business.'

'I was only asking!' I reply, frowning back. I thought Juan had stopped all his moodiness now we were here, but clearly not. 'I meant with the arrows. What's happening with them?'

'We are going to catch a pig,' he answers, nodding to his uncle next to him, who's now stretching and bending the bow part of a bow and arrow.

'To eat?' I ask.

'We'll try and catch two. One for us to eat, and one to trade with the fishermen. That's how my family survive – trading meat and vegetables with the fishermen who go past on their trips to and from Brazil.'

'Do you think any of the fishermen who pass will know how Auntie Marg is?' I ask hopefully, pouncing on his words. 'Some of them might be coming from Iquitos!'

'Maybe, but I haven't told my family you may have killed your auntie. I wanted them to like you,' Juan replies matter-of-factly.

'Oh. Right. So . . . why do they think I'm here?' I ask, partly relieved.

'I said you were a tourist and really wanted to see the jungle, and that's why you're constantly taking photos on your phone. I also said that you might give them a big tip when you leave,' he adds.

I panic. 'But you know I haven't got any money!'

'Well then, you had better be helpful,' he says, but there's a hint of a smile on his face. 'Anyway, my family don't really deal in money. They will swap vegetables or meat for coffee, sugar or rice. I had packed some in my boat, but SOMEONE threw them out. Sometimes my aunts make and trade beads or bows and arrows for the fishermen to sell in tourist towns like Leticia – but a pig would be worth more.'

'So – those arrows,' I say, nodding at them. 'Are they to trade? Or to use to catch the pig?'

'These are to trade. To sell to the tourists,' Juan tells me, placing the pile of narrow spikes by his feet. 'These' – he pauses for dramatic effect as he picks up a thick spear with a sharp silver blade welded to the end – 'are for hunting.'

'*Vámonos*,' Juan's uncle tells him, and they pass the bag of smaller arrows to one of the kids. Juan and his uncle grab a hunting spear each, then turn and head into the jungle.

Juan didn't ask if I wanted to come, but I grab the remaining spear and follow anyway. It looks more interesting than playing with little kids. Juan's moving quickly, probably to try and shake me off, but within minutes we're deep in the jungle and I don't know my way back so my only option is to keep up.

We slip through the curtain of trees into the thickness of the forest, layer upon layer of green with golden highlights, and in seconds my face and body are soaking wet, a combination of sweat and jungle moisture.

They navigate the trees, bushes and roots with ease, stepping on branches and spiky thorn-like twigs without even blinking. I'm barefoot, and although my feet have hardened to the jungle over the last few days, stubbing my toe and catching my feet on sharp twigs and spiky leaves still hurts. Juan frowns at me, his lips pursed every time I gasp and wince.

'Shhh!' hisses Juan in my direction. He and his uncle are a few paces ahead, heads high, both sniffing the air.

'Shouldn't we be looking down? Looking for tracks?' I whisper. I've actually done this before. Well, obviously I haven't looked for pigs in a jungle before, but when Gav and I used to play cops and robbers I always tracked him down by looking for his footprints in the farmyard mud, and the squidgy brown jungle ground is covered in countless tracks and prints too. I give the air an experimental sniff – and then I understand why they're doing it: it's a bit like horse, a bit like cow, but it's definitely poo, and I'm standing in it! It's almost ankle-deep, clogged between my toes, and it STINKS! Wriggling my toes releases even more of the smell, and it's warm, so the pig must be close.

Something cold taps me lightly on the arm, as Juan gets my attention with his spear. He nods ahead and I follow his stare. Sure enough, snorting and sniffing at the ground of a small clearing through the trees is a pig. But it's not like the ones we have on the farm – this one has a long nose, its belly is further off the ground and it's almost entirely black in colour.

Juan and his uncle make signals to each other, using just their fingers. In an instant, they are charging, galloping over bushes in the direction of the pig. Not knowing what to do, I race after them, the silence broken by the crashing of footsteps and snapping of branches around us.

Juan's good arm, lean and muscly, is raised above his head. He throws it forward, catapulting the spear. There's a squeal, a crash, but the pig is still moving. He must have scratched it, because the pig is screaming as if in pain, squealing the highest pitched squeal I have EVER heard. My heart is racing so fast I can hear the blood thundering through my veins, as if someone's banging a drum inside my ear.

Juan's adding to the noise, yelling at me: 'OI OI OI!' Juan and his uncle chase it on, but I stop. I can hear the pig limping around, trying to get away from Juan and his uncle, the thundering crash of trotters on twigs getting nearer and closing in on me. I stand with my feet wide and my grip firm. The trees are packed, dark and tight around me.

Its hair scratches against my calf as it tries to wriggle by, squealing and squeaking. Juan and his uncle aren't close enough. Quickly, I close my eyes, raise the spear and push it down.

Juan is on his knees beside me in seconds. His blade is on the pig's neck, and the wriggling and scratching of thick skin against my leg stops. Its body is heavy and hot. It collapses against me and I buckle.

Silence.

I gulp. The spear is still in my hand, but my grip is no longer firm and my hands are shaking and sweating. I'm panting, trying to catch my breath, as if gulps of oxygen will help me to make sense of what I've just done.

Dear Gav,

Remember when Dad told us about that sheep
he had to put out of its misery because it had
broken its leg? We said he should have kept
it alive, but he said it's cruel to let an animal
suffer, and if they're badly injured it's better for
them to be killed? Well, do you think the same
thing applies to pigs? I mean, do you think it's
OK to kill a pig if it's already been injured?

Juan and his uncle were going to hunt a pig, so
I went along. First the pig got injured because
Juan missed. He threw his spear and it only
hurt the pig, but it was making lots of noise, so
I think it was in a lot of pain. Then I heard it running towards me, so I finished it off and put it
out of its misery. But now I feel really guilty.

The second pig we caught was a lot more
straightforward. It didn't suffer, and Juan said
it's OK, because they haven't caught any for
weeks, and we caught two really big ones,
which means: a) Juan's family can sell one for
a good price, and keep the second one and get
lots of meat from it; and b) they were probably
the oldest in their family, so were most likely to

die soon anyway. Do you think that makes it OK?

The only problem was, we then had to carry them back, one at a time because they were so heavy. We tied their feet together and Juan took one end, and his uncle took the other, and I carried the spears behind them. That bit was awful, because I felt like both pigs were staring at me the whole time, their eyes wide open and their tongues hanging out. The smell was awful – hot, muddy pigs mixed with blood and sweat. I pretended I wasn't bothered but I think Eva could tell, because she took the spears straight off me as soon as we got back and led me round to the other side of the house to have a wash and play with Eric.

Don't worry about Marg. She's here some-where, snapping away. Snap, snap, snap – you know her. SERIOUSLY – do not worry about her.

Love

Amy
x

CHAPTER 23

'*He dances in the flames, laughing at the pain that would make others cry. He comes and goes in the night, impossible to pin down, impossible to know how long he will be around . . .*'

Juan whispers in my ear, translating the story being told by one of the prettiest girls in the group. The smallest kids are staring up at her from the ground where they are sitting. The fire beside them crackles and spits, throwing shadows across their faces, making it hard to work out whether they are scared or excited. Either way they are hooked, hanging on the story-teller's every word. She's speaking quietly in fast, fluent Spanish, but she hasn't seen Juan creep between the shadows to her side.

I hear the words *Saci pererê* again, and then she stops. Her expression is awkward as she sees Juan, and he

217

lifts his left hand up in front of his face, revealing the stretched, burned white skin, the folds illuminated by the fire.

There's a collective intake of breath. The girl is silent. One of the little kids scrambles to his feet. He runs towards the house as Juan bursts out laughing. Then an adult voice booms from the house and the group lets out a sigh again, only this time it's a mix of relief and frustration.

'It's time to eat,' Juan tells me.

Juan's uncles and aunties have cooked the smaller of the two pigs caught earlier today. Juan killed the one we're about to eat. It was easier to catch than mine. It pretty much ran straight up to him. Mine will be traded for sugar and coffee with the passing fishermen. I was so happy when Juan's uncle told everyone what I did. I felt like everyone looked at me differently then. The men patted me on the back, and even the ones who haven't spoken to me before smiled and nodded. Juan's pig is hanging upside down with its feet tied together, a bit like you see in the films. I still feel weird about my part in its capture, but it smells *amazing*. Juicy slices of meat are being cut off with a huge knife, and Juan's aunt hands around plates of vegetables, lots of orangy-looking potatoes, and trays of sliced bananas with berries and nuts.

'Smile!' I say, snapping away with my phone. The feast, the flames, the faces – I'm getting some brilliant photos, if I do say so myself.

'*Gracias*,' I say to Eva as she hands me a plate of food. I try to roll my 'r' like they all do, but I might have gone a bit over the top.

She smiles at me and says shyly in English, 'You are welcome.' I see her catch Juan's eye and I guess he's been teaching her a few phrases.

I wish I could use that translation app to work out how to say much more in Spanish, but my phone battery is really low now and I'm trying only to use it for taking photos. 'Do you go to, er . . .' I hesitate, trying to think what the word for 'school' might be. 'Schoolo?'

Juan snorts with laughter. '*Al colegio*,' he says.

'*Al colegio?*' I repeat.

Eva smiles and shakes her head.

I try another question. 'Where is your . . .' I think, making sure I've got it right this time. '*Madre?*' I try.

Eva's smile falls from her face. She looks at me and shakes her head sadly.

'I'm sorry,' I say, wishing I could take back the words, but at the same time feeling more curious than ever. 'Juan, how do you say "I'm sorry" in Spanish?'

'*Lo siento,*' Juan says gruffly.

'*Lo siento,*' I repeat, looking at them both.

'It's OK,' says Juan. 'It . . . happened a long time ago.' His words are flat and I suddenly understand that he wasn't just being moody with me when I brought his family up before: something terrible must have happened.

'What happened?' I ask softly.

Juan hesitates. He shrugs, his eyes staring at the floor. I don't push it. I know not to ask again so for once, I stay silent. I wait for him to speak.

'It all changed when they came to build roads,' he tells me. 'My mother and father, aunts and uncles – all of us, we lived much further into the jungle. We were a big community, lots of other families too. Then *they* arrived . . .' His words tail off as the elderly lady who the little ones call *cuca* comes over to push more meat onto Juan's plate. He smiles, nods and waits for her to shuffle away again before he continues.

'Who came? What roads?' I ask.

'Men who worked for a big, rich company,' Juan explains. 'They came to cut down trees to make roads.' He smiles. 'Well, they *tried*, but they learned that it's very hard to cut down trees and make a path in the forest. These trees have been growing for ever, and . . . it disturbs things. It disturbs nature.'

'What do you mean?' I ask, knitting my eyebrows – Juan is so mysterious and cryptic. Again, I bite my tongue to stop myself firing off all the questions I want to ask. Be patient, Amy, I tell myself.

'We look after the forest and it looks after us,' Juan says. 'We respect it. It respects us. That is what we believe, that is what my family believes.'

I'm lost, but I wait for him to go on.

'The men who came to cut down the trees wanted to give all the families money so that we would move out of the area. All the others agreed, but my family said they did not want to leave. All of my family, that is, except for my father.'

'Dudu wanted to leave?' I ask.

Juan nodded. 'He said that they would cut down the trees whether we stayed or whether we left. He said that we should leave while we still could.' He sighs. 'My father had worked on tourist boats, and he had learned to speak English. He thought we could have a better life in a town like Iquitos.' He's speaking so quietly now that I have to lean in to him to hear what he's saying. 'My mother wanted to ask the men to stop. She believed that they might listen to us.' He shakes his head. 'She went to them. She warned them that cutting down so many trees would anger the forest. She believed that *el tunchi*, or the sirens – all those stories – exist for a reason: to stop people doing things like this. She was worried and she was just trying to help them. She was like that.

'But they laughed at her. They thought she was talking nonsense and just trying to scare them.' Anger creeps into his voice. 'Some of them were sick: one had a cough, another a fever. Nothing serious, but they were illnesses my mother had never had before. She was vulnerable to their germs, and she fell ill soon after. She was not like my father – she had never visited Iquitos or another town, had never met many other people, had never travelled far. So she caught their sickness.

'She did not want to visit a doctor, and she . . . she died. Slowly. In pain. Those men, they *killed* her.' The last few words merge into one another as they tumble from his mouth, as if Juan's desperate to get them out as quickly as he can.

I don't know what to say. For once I am searching my brain for the words rather than biting my tongue to stop them. 'I'm so sorry, Juan. That's horrible.'

Juan nods.

'What about your dad?' I ask. 'Dudu?'

'He was right,' Juan says. 'The men cut the trees down anyway, without giving my family any money. My family had to move here, closer to the river, where my uncles could trade with the fishermen. My father was so very angry. Angry about what happened to my mother. Angry that we lost our home. He was frightened that more of us would fall sick. Then he felt so guilty about . . .' He glances down at his scarred hand, his voice trailing off.

I'm amazed at how much Juan has just told me and I don't want him to stop now. I risk a question, looking at the floor as I ask: 'About what? What, Juan?'

Juan shakes his head. 'Nothing. Anyway, that is when he decided to leave. He was too angry here. Eva wanted to stay with the rest of the family. But I decided to go with him, learn to speak English in Iquitos. I—'

'Juan!'

Juan's uncle, the one we hunted the pigs with, interrupts us. '*Ya es la hora,*' he says quietly, ignoring me and Eva and looking only at Juan. '*Lo antes posible. Mañana por la noche?*'

Juan gets up and heads straight outside with his uncle, retreating into the shadows where they whisper together. I stare after him, more confused than ever. What's going on?

Mañana? Doesn't that mean 'tomorrow'? What's Juan going to do with his uncle tomorrow?

Eva shakes her head. A look I know well creeps across her face; Mam does it too. She is angry, and worried.

I know he's up to something she won't like, but I don't know what.

CHAPTER 24

Lying snugly in my hammock with a bellyful of pork, gently swaying with birds crooning overhead, I realize I'm starting to feel a bit dizzy. Everyone, including me, went to bed hours ago, only I haven't fallen asleep yet. My head is full of questions about Juan. He's so secretive. What is he up to? Why is his hand like that?

My stomach starts to ache, then to throb, then to burn. I can't do anything other than lie here, so I hold my breath, biting my tongue when the agonizing cramps grip my stomach. I don't want to wake everyone, I don't want to make a fuss, but I don't think I can stifle this pain for much longer. Actually, I don't think I *am* managing to be quiet after all. A groan gurgles up my throat and out of my mouth, a pain-filled yelp that brings Tía Antonia into the room.

I'm in agony. My forehead and hands are damp with sweat. My hammock and clothes are soaking. Placing my hands on my belly, I can feel that it's swollen up like a balloon.

Tía Antonia spots my screwed-up face and comes close, wearing a questioning expression, especially when she sees me touching my tummy.

'*Le duele?*' she asks. I think she's asking what's wrong, and her voice is so soft I want to squeal for my mam. I feel awful, but I can't explain it. Juan's the only one who can speak English.

Another agonizing pain grips my stomach. I shake my head stubbornly, trying to blink back the tears. 'There's nothing the matter with me. I just need a minute,' I say hoarsely as she leans closer, reaching out to touch my head. She calls for Eva and Juan, concern on her face and in her voice.

Moments later Juan walks into the room, rubbing sleep from his eyes. His auntie speaks quietly and quickly, gesturing to my swollen stomach. 'What did you eat?' he asks.

'Nothing,' I manage. 'Nothing different from

anyone else. Just berries and fish, then the pork tonight.'

Juan frowns, and his auntie says something else. 'Did you . . . where have you been going to . . . you know?' he says.

'I didn't go in the river, if that's what you mean!' I say indignantly. 'I know about those fish that swim up inside you.'

'So, the shed?' Juan says.

'No,' I answer. 'I went in the forest. That plank is too narrow – and everyone can see where I'm going and I don't like it. There's a huge tree with big swollen roots that's perfect, so I've been using that.'

Juan translates what I've said to Tía Antonia, who's looking at me now in disbelief.

I don't get it. I needed to go, so I went. I often go outside at home – not on the front doorstep or anything, but in the fields, behind the bushes. It saves going inside. Taking your trainers off and all that. Mam calls it wild weeing.

'What's wrong? Can't I go there?' I ask.

Juan shakes his head. His auntie's now moving as if someone has pressed fast-forward. She's calling out of the door, grabbing every grown-up she can find, waving her arms, talking quickly, frantic foreign words tumbling out of her mouth. She's using the same word again and again, and all the time more of Juan's aunties and uncles and cousins are coming to stare at my swelling, burning stomach.

It might actually burst, it's so painful. I can't believe this is happening to me – I'm never going to get home! I'm going to *die* here! Gavin will get my room and everything. I'll never be able to explain that what happened to Auntie Marg was an accident.

There's a lot of rushing around and knocking things over, but my head stays buried in the cocoon of the hammock. I don't want to catch anyone's eye, see anyone looking at me like I'm stupid; the glare of disappointment I'm so used to. Eva sits close to me, holding my hand in hers, and even Juan looks worried. 'One of my uncles is going to go in the motorboat to fetch the shaman,' he tells me.

'The what?'

'The shaman. Like . . . a doctor. He knows everything.'

'What did I do? What's happening to me?' I croak.

Juan looks at me. 'That tree is very special to us,' he explains. 'It is sacred. It is called *la lupuna.*'

That's the word I keep hearing.

'We believe that if you disrespect *la lupuna* or the forest, it will have its revenge on you,' Juan continues.

I remember the TV show I watched with Gav and Auntie Marg, and the words and pictures on my Top Trumps card.

La lupuna – the sacred tree.

I did a number two on it.

TOP TRUMPS

LA LUPUNA

Large trees found within the jungle, believed to have a spirit that exists to protect the rainforest. Those who upset the tree will and do suffer.

Appearance:

Huge imposing trees that grow up to 10 metres wide. Branches tend to be high up with the trunk showing one swollen, or belly-like, section.

Top strength:

Some believe the tree has almost magical spell-like abilities to make those who disrespect it suffer.

Most likely to be found:

Deep in the rainforest, among lots of dense trees, flora and fauna. Identifiable by its swollen belly.

Deadly?

It is not known for sure if *la lupuna* can cause actual death, but certainly there have been many reports of the pain and suffering the spirit of the tree can bring about.

SCARE RATING: 42 • DANGER RATING: 61 • COOL RATING: 70

Dear Gav,

Quick one. I love you all. Mam and Bob especially, but even you. I don't want to be a sop, but I don't ever say it, so just in case anything happens to me I want you to know I wouldn't swap you for anyone. Well, maybe a millionaire pilot who could fly me home in a private jet, but other than that I would not swap any of you.

Amy
x

PS. Not that anything will happen to me. Just saying, in case, you know.
PPS. Auntie Marg is fine. If you haven't heard from her, it's because she is BUSY, that is all. NOTHING is wrong.

CHAPTER 25

The little ones were getting so traumatized by my groans and moans last night that Tía Antonia and Juan moved me to a hammock on the front porch. It's cooler here and although my stomach feels worse, the breeze is amazing. From here I can see the sky. My eyelids are heavy and my head is spinning, but as the sun starts to creep above the horizon, pushing the blackness from the sky, I hear the buzz of a motorboat coming towards the house.

Birds chirp and flap their wings, making way for our guest: the shaman. The grown-ups murmur and twitter in their own way, and there's a ripple of excitement about whoever's going to turn up. I can't sit up to see because my stomach is too swollen, but I don't have to wait long.

Feet swoosh through the long grass as our much-anticipated visitor makes his way to the house. Then there are heavy steps along the porch towards my hammock, and I can hear necklaces jangling and bangles clinking as a heavy shadow is cast across me.

The most striking man I have ever seen is standing over me. I hold my breath as his tanned face comes closer to mine. The whites of his eyes are bright, and every inch of his face is covered in swirly red paint. He has a huge nose and a serious expression. His face is framed by thick black hair, with a row of red feathers on the top of his head. Yellow, green and red beads are piled around his neck and shoulders, and he isn't wearing a top, but he has a strange, fluffy white skirt on. He looks – well, beautiful. Can you say that about a man?

With all Juan's family gathered around, the shaman kneels by my hammock and gives me a cup full to the brim of a sticky, stinky, clear juice. He holds it to my mouth and I take a sip. I almost spit it out, it tastes so bad, but out of the corner of my eye I can see Eva nodding encouragingly, so I swallow it down. I hate taking medicine but anything's got to be better than the pain I'm in now.

I don't know what's in the cup, but almost immediately it makes me feel like my head is heavy, so heavy I have to lay it back down.

Hours must pass before I wake up again, because I can tell from the dim light that it's almost dusk. I haven't moved all day. My stomach is feeling better; the swelling's gone down.

Slowly, groggily, I sit up, trying not to lose my balance and fall out of the hammock. I am starving. I head for the main room with the table and there's a bowl of those yummy berries sitting there. One of the aunties gestures to me to eat, and I take a handful, then another and another. I can't believe I feel so much better.

'What was in that sticky stuff I drank?' I ask Juan as he joins me in the kitchen.

'The shaman went to the tree and apologized on your behalf. He cut into its belly and the liquid came out. That is what you drank.'

'And that's what stopped my stomach exploding?' I rub my belly gently.

'Now that you can walk again, you must go to the tree and apologize yourself,' Juan continues.

I stare at him. 'What? Say sorry to a tree?'

'Why are you arguing? Do you want to be ill again? It's simple. Apologize, and the balance will be back to normal. Show the tree you respect it,' Juan says, matter-of-factly.

'But – well, the thing is . . .' I sigh, embarrassed, but more relieved. I've actually run out of arguments. 'Fine, let's get it over with.'

Awkwardly I follow Juan out of the house and through the bushes to *la lupuna*. So this is considered magical and sacred? It *is* a cool tree, I suppose, towering above me, almost the size of a house. Just its roots are as big as some of the biggest trees I have ever seen, stretching from the soil. Its swollen-looking belly has a gash in it where the shaman must have cut into its bark.

I feel my cheeks burn. I can't believe I'm about to speak to a tree.

'Er . . . sorry,' I mutter. 'I won't do it again.'

I glance at Juan. He's not saying a word, but I swear he's biting back a grin.

'Er, tree . . . would it be OK if I take your picture?' Now I feel *really* stupid. Obviously there's silence from the tree. How did I expect it to react? 'I'll just take one photo, just to show my family how amazing you are!' I add, cringing. I can't believe I've just apologized *and* sucked up to a tree.

Even more than before, I know how out of my depth I am here. I can put on a brave face and try and convince myself I could live here if I had to, but the truth is, I probably couldn't.

I step back, crouch down and take the widest, highest photograph I can of the dark, towering roots. I need a photo of this, and brilliant – I can see, flicking through the last few, that Juan got a picture of the shaman.

'Thanks, Juan!' I say, acknowledging the photo.

'Go back to the hammock and get some more sleep,' he replies, nodding at the house. 'I'm heading out in the motorboat early this evening, as I need to take care of some business.'

'What?' I pounce on his words.

Juan shakes his head. 'Nothing for you to know about. I will be back later.'

'Is it whatever you keep sneaking off to talk to your uncle about?'

A flash of concern crosses his face, but he masks it well.

'I know you're up to something. It's obvious!' I add. 'Is it something to do with those people you didn't want to be seen by? You told me it was important that no one knew you were around.' My mind's racing, trying to remember all the clues he's accidentally dropped, to piece together the mutterings and work out what he's up to.

Juan sighs. He knows I'm onto him.

'Maybe I'll just ask Eva?' I tease.

Juan pauses, then shakes his head. 'You don't speak enough Spanish to ask her,' he says nervously. 'You'll only upset her. Don't, OK?' There's panic in his voice.

I say nothing. I don't want to upset her, but then I don't think Juan has any right to hide stuff from me. I'm involved now, whether he likes it or not.

I follow him as he stomps towards the house.

'I think I *will* go straight to bed after all,' I say as Juan looks at me suspiciously. I head to my hammock, grabbing another handful of berries on my way, and turn to see Juan walking towards his uncle. Our eyes meet as Juan's uncle pulls Juan against him, their heads close so I can't hear what is being whispered.

While they're deep in discussion I slip back out of the house and creep towards the motorboat. I'll hide in here until he goes, and then I'll find out what he's up to.

It's cluttered inside, with rope, a blue plastic sheet, some buckets – *none* of which I am touching or removing. Stepping aboard, the vessel rocks under my feet and I land on one of the buckets awkwardly. I get under the plastic sheet and out of sight. It's so uncomfortable under here. What's he got all this rubbish for anyway? I hope it's not long until Juan comes and we set off to wherever we're going.

I wait a while, and I can see through the tiny rips in this sheet that it's properly dark now. It's so hot here. I'm sweating, and my knees are folded uncomfortably underneath me as I try to make myself as small and invisible as possible. I hear footsteps approaching the boat and hold my breath in case I make something move. I feel Juan jumping inside and pushing us away from the shore.

At first we move slowly, then we surge forward. It's hard to work out which way we're going as I sit curled up with my head between my knees. My stomach still isn't completely fixed and I'm regretting all the berries I ate when I got up earlier. I probably shouldn't have had so many . . . I can taste them in the back of my throat. Oh no . . . I feel sick – really sick. I get that watery feeling in my mouth when your tongue and teeth feel wet, when you feel the sick gurgling at the back of your throat and there's no way to stop it . . .

I clap my hands over my mouth and in a gut-wrenching second I throw up all over myself, sick squeezing its way between my fingers and spilling down my front. *Yuck!*

The blue plastic sheet is ripped from my head and I'm face to face with Juan. There's a look of horror on his face, and his eyes are as white and round as the moon glowing above his head.

'What are you doing here?' he bellows. 'Why are you *always* hiding in a boat when I don't want you there! And why are you—' He stares at me. 'You *stink*!'

'You're *so* selfish!' I retort, feeling seriously sorry for myself. 'I only want to know what you're up to! You've been plotting something ever since we set off from Iquitos! You tell me a few details and then you bite my head off. It's only right that you tell me what's going on. Why did you really come here? It wasn't just to see your sister and your auntie, was it? Juan!?'

A half-frustrated scream, half-grunt rumbles from Juan. His fists and jaw are clenched. '*Otra vez usted está aquí!*' he spits, his expression angry. 'You'll have to sit in the boat and not move and never, *ever* speak of this, Amy. I mean it. This is serious,' he warns me. 'If the loggers found out it was me trying to scare them away—'

'What? Loggers? You mean – the ones that caused your mam to get sick? We're getting revenge, aren't we?' I squeal. My feet jiggle with nerves. It's exciting – OK, a bit scary, but in a good way. Adrenaline runs through my veins.

Juan nods. 'I can't go back now. Once Eva realizes I've gone, she will be angry with me, and if I take you back she won't let me leave again. I must do this tonight. Tonight is the full moon – enough light for me to do what I need to without a torch that might wake the security guards. Promise me you won't cause trouble or mess things up. Don't do what you normally do!'

'Well, that's not very fair—' I begin to argue, only his stare stops me in my tracks. Maybe I will just shut up.

The moon is high in the sky, lighting our path across the dark water. We sit in silence. It feels cold for the first time since we got here, and I hug my arms into my body for warmth.

'How far away is it?' I whisper after an hour or so has passed.

Juan hasn't spoken once. He's barely even looked at me. Instead he's sat staring ahead, one hand on the little engine propelling us forward. It's low and quiet so we move slowly, but even that is enough to fill the air with the smell of petrol.

'The work site is ahead,' says Juan, his jaw and arms highlighted in the bright moonlight. 'They cut down the trees miles inland, but up here on the riverbank is where they saw them into pieces, before they transport them by river.'

Several huge barn-like buildings creep into sight. Juan switches off the engine so we glide the rest of the way in silence, neither of us speaking. I'm too nervous to speak anyway. There's just the occasional sound of the paddle meeting the water as Juan propels us forward. He knows exactly where he's going.

'Have you been here before?' I ask.

'Yes. They have different sites, they rob different parts of the jungle for different trees, but this one has been here for months,' he explains, looking straight ahead. 'These people do not need to know I am here,' he adds.

I study his face. 'What are you going to do?' I ask. The serious look on his face is starting to scare me. 'You're not going to . . . to hurt anyone?' I try to add a sarcastic chuckle to my question. I can't believe I am asking this.

'No.' Juan shakes his head. 'They just need to be reminded that these trees aren't theirs to take. Chopping them down affects the jungle, everyone and everything that lives here, and there should be consequences for the loggers too.'

He expertly guides the boat into an inlet, jumps out silently and ties the boat to a tree. Reaching back into the boat he pulls out a big metal drum, the contents sloshing around heavily. I follow him as quietly as I can.

Juan points towards one of the huge structures facing the river. There are no doors and the moon is so bright that I can see inside: piles of wooden planks stacked neatly. The flash on my camera phone highlights the leaves closest to us, with everything in the background picked out by the moon. Juan shakes his head. 'No flash,' he hisses.

Occasionally someone, or something, heckles us from the tree tops. Juan doesn't flinch but I jump every time, my heart leaping further up my throat. In between the heckles, it's intimidatingly silent. Even my breath feels too loud.

Juan is picking his way through the bushes to the largest shed. I'm making much slower progress than him: for once I can *not* be a bull in a china shop. Juan is so calm and quiet, I HAVE to be the same.

I approach the building, pressing my body tightly against the cold, rusty corrugated tin wall. Inside I can see that Juan's climbing into the cab of a huge machine like a tractor. He takes the keys from the ignition and slides them quickly into his back pocket. Then he leaps from the cabin and starts picking up saws and hammers, piling them into his arms and carrying them towards me. He thrusts a heavy pile into my arms. 'In the river!' he hisses. 'Drop them in! The current will take them miles away.'

Too scared to argue, I do as I'm told. Juan is a man on a mission.

I head back to Juan, who's unscrewed the cap of the metal drum. He's pouring thick black liquid all over the floor of the building, a trail snaking its way round the piles of wood and up the steps of the tractor to its cabin, and all over the seat and dash-board inside. I can't believe this. I've seen it in films – the bad guys pour petrol everywhere and then light a match and the whole place explodes and there's always someone behind the flames, screaming. I can't let this happen!

I throw myself at Juan, trying to grab the drum

from his hand. Catching him by surprise, it falls to the ground as if in slow motion. Thick, gloopy liquid creeps from its neck all over the floor.

Juan's eyes are nearly popping out of his head. 'What are you *doing*?' he hisses.

'What am *I* doing? You nutter! You can't set fire to this building. You'll kill people, you idiot!' I snap.

'What are you talking about?' he asks in disbelief, shaking his head. 'Fire?'

His voice trails off. I don't know where to look. 'So . . . it's not petrol?' I say, looking at the black liquid on the floor.

'No! It's just dye, from a tree bark. A rotten one, so it will stain everything and make this place stink like dead, rotting fish,' Juan explains. 'Starting a fire would damage the jungle, and quickly get out of control. But I will do anything I can to spook them, to let them know they are not welcome.'

I look around, starting to understand. I feel so sad for Juan. 'Maybe it will never work,' he adds, as if he can read my mind. 'But I'm angry at them, I'm angry at what has happened to my family . . . and I have to keep trying.'

'This is why your family call you that name – *Saci Pererê*. Isn't it?' I ask.

'Yes. It means "trickster",' Juan explains.

I nod. This is all making sense now. 'I really thought you were going to set it all on fire,' I admit.

Juan shakes his head. 'I hate them – but I would never burn the place. That's how—'

He glances down at his hand, and suddenly I understand. I thought it looked like it had been melted, burned. I knew it. 'That's how you hurt your hand, isn't it? Juan, what happened?' I ask. I'm partly asking because – well, I'm curious and nosy and I have to know. But also, Mam always says a problem shared is a problem halved, and this is obviously a big problem.

Juan takes a few deep, long breaths. 'The people who work here all have guns, huge guns, so although we blamed them for my mother's death, we knew we could not fight them. But we wanted to try to scare them away in a different way. We played tricks on them. Bad tricks.

'One night, when my mother was already ill, we came here and one man had left out a water flask. My father put some crushed-up berries in it. They are not poisonous, but they make you see things – things that aren't really there. My father hid in the bushes to watch and I climbed a tree. We thought the men would share the flask among them, and it might scare them – but they didn't. One man drank it all.

'He thought he saw something on the other side of the river – a woman. He waded straight into the water, but it was too strong and fast. My father saw that he was going to drown, and he couldn't let the man die, so he dragged him to safety. Then he tried to get away before the others could catch him, and he shouted to me to hurry up and get back to the boat.'

Juan pauses for a moment, remembering. 'Until my father shouted for me, they didn't know I was there too – but when they realized there was someone else in the trees, they began setting fire to anything that would light. There had been no rain for days so the trees caught fire quickly. The whole place started crackling and creaking in the heat. I sat in the top of the tree, watching the flames get closer. I could smell the fire, but I could not move – I don't know why. I was frozen. My father was screaming for me to jump, but I clung to the branch, so terrified I did not even realize the tree I was in was now alight. Then I was on fire too.'

He holds his hand up; the hand that has fascinated me for days. The hand that doesn't seem to hurt, but clearly causes him pain.

'I don't know if I jumped or fell. I landed badly, but I managed to get into the water before the men caught me.'

'And then what?' I ask, desperate to know what happened.

Juan takes a deep breath. His shoulders rise and fall. 'My father dragged me into the boat and we went home. Eva sat with me when she could, but my mother needed her more. Each day I got a little bit better . . . and each day she got a little bit worse.'

'And since she died,' I say, 'you keep coming back here to try and get rid of the loggers?'

'Eva and Tía Antonia hate it,' explains Juan. 'They don't want me to do these things – they worry that it's dangerous and pointless. They think the *Saci Pererê* nickname will encourage me! But I don't do it because of the nickname – I do it because I owe it to my mother. I need to show my family I support them and I haven't forgotten them, especially now that I don't live here any more.'

He nods at the phone in the case around my neck. 'You could do something too,' he says. 'Take some photographs. People like this are tearing the Amazon apart. You could show people when you go back home.'

I nod and grab my phone. He's right, and I can see why he's so upset. This is where his family have lived for generations, and it's being butchered.

'Come on,' Juan adds, tugging at my arm. 'I'll show you the rest.'

For the next hour or so, Juan leads me through the jungle. The shadows, creaks and groans from the canopy seem more intimidating than ever. I step where Juan steps, picking my way over felled logs and branches until our path becomes less tight and narrow. The noises become more distant, the moon much brighter. We're heading towards a huge clearing, and it smells different here, like the shed on our farm where my dad chops up firewood and stores his tools. A hint of petrol.

'They have industrial-sized chainsaws. They can take down ten trees in half a day,' Juan says, still pacing ahead and walking further into the clearing.

Metres of what looks like wasteland stretch before me. Trees have been snapped from their roots. Bark and branches reach out of the ground. We're so exposed to the moonlight here that we can see everything. It's eerie here, because it's oddly quiet. There are no birds, no creatures scuttling around. The silence is creepy – it's like a graveyard.

I take photo after photo. The piles of sawdust where trees have been sawn down. The detail on the tree stumps that have been brutally hacked away. The roots ripped from the ground. The cigarette butts peppered among the trampled shoots and roots poking from the dusty ground.

Juan wanders among the debris of the fallen trees and broken branches, picking bits up and putting them down again, vaguely attempting to tidy something that would take years to put right. After a little while we head back into the warm, dense, noisy part of the jungle. Neither of us are speaking. Both of us are haunted.

Back in the boat, it's hard to know what to say. I know now why Juan was so weird when I asked him about his family. I understand why he doesn't want to live here, too. In some ways it would be so cool. He wouldn't have to go to school, for starters. He could basically play out all day – it's like one long summer holiday for his cousins. But I don't think I would want to be here all the time. Thinking about my mam; missing her all the time.

I remember how much I hated our first night in the jungle, with all the noises echoing above our heads, but I realize how much I've grown to like it, and how angry I feel about what's being done to it. Those sounds are reassuring, like they're reminding us that we're not alone, and maybe that's a good thing.

'Juan – those noises, the ones we've been hearing ever since that first night on the river,' I say. 'Is it really *el tunchi*?'

Juan smiles.

'*El tunchi* may be real, or it may not be,' he says. 'But the sounds you can hear – they are definitely not *el tunchi*. Those are howler monkeys!'

HOWLER MONKEY

One of the largest monkeys and loudest animals in the Amazon.

Appearance:

Adults can grow to about 90 cm, and weigh up to 10 kg. Their tail is long and strong and can stretch another 90 cm. Their fur is black and their necks and jaws are large.

Top strength:

Their incredible voice. Male howlers use their howl to defend their turf, and their roar or distant groan can be heard for miles through dense forest. Their tails act as a fifth limb, having the ability to grip trees and branches.

Most likely to be found:

Look out for raining seeds or streams of wee. The howlers like to sit high in the tree canopy where the leaves are youngest. You may not be able to see them but often visitors report being peed on from up high. That's a howler! They get all the water they need from the fruit, nuts and flowers they eat so rarely leave the treetops unless they need to look for extra water. Live in groups of 15–20 monkeys.

Deadly?

No, but highly entertaining.

SCARE RATING: 32 • DANGER RATING: 33 • COOL RATING: 86

CHAPTER 26

Two mornings later, Juan and I are packing up the little motorboat to leave. Counting the water bottles and shifting the buckets of fruit to keep us fed and watered on our return journey to Iquitos, I can't help but feel anxious. I'm excited to be going back, keen to get one step closer to my family, but I am so nervous about Auntie Marg.

In a bid to keep my mind off this yesterday, Juan taught me to climb trees like he and his family do. Like Spider-Man does. Using a vine to loop around the back of the tree, you get your feet flat against the bark, and you can shuffle up without even a branch for leverage. It was amazing – I felt like we were miles above the forest floor! But all I wanted to do was show Gavin. Not just to show off – I wished he was there so that I could teach him to do it too. I knew then that it was time to go.

I'll miss everyone, though. I've been with Juan for a week now, and with his family for several days. They've been so nice to me. They're all definitely less suspicious of me now. They aren't my family, but they've treated me like they are.

'Put that spare paddle in!' orders Juan. 'We have a working engine again, but you're on board, so anything could happen.' He smirks.

'You'll be glad I came with you when Auntie Marg gives these photos to a paper and those loggers are punished properly,' I reply. 'People go mad for eco-stuff. She'll make a real fuss for you. I will too.'

Most of the family have come to wave us off. They've put a smear of red face paint across each of my cheeks – for good luck, apparently. I still don't know what most of them are saying, but they all smile, so I do too. Eric is here too, scampering around the kids' legs. He's going to stay here as he's made lots of new friends, and I can't take him back to where we found him. He'll be happy here, and well looked after. I know it's right for him, but I'll still miss him.

I think I'll miss it here too. The kids giggle constantly as we load the boat up and get ready to leave, unafraid of the bugs and beasts that crawl across their little toes. They play in the river and in the rainforest. Even though they don't have a single iPad, they never get bored and they never have to go to school. Everyone seems so fit, too – they're awake from the moment the sun comes up, cooking, laughing and fishing, collecting berries, leaping effortlessly over knotted vines and branches in the jungle. It's so different.

Our moonlight adventure hasn't been mentioned, but a couple of Juan's uncles patted him on the back yesterday morning. Tía Antonia has tears in her eyes when she says goodbye to Juan, and she gives me a big hug.

Eva squeezes my hand tightly, and gives me a present: a necklace made out of colourful beads. I try to say, '*Gracias*' but my voice goes all croaky and tight.

We hop in the boat, Juan starts it up and we push off. 'Thank you! *Gracias!*' I yell as the house and the people slide out of view.

I might never see them again, and that thought

prompts a tear. Maybe I could pop back next holidays. I could print some of the photos I took this time and bring them. Then again, it was quite a long flight.

I ponder. Hang on – flights.

'Juan, what day is it?' I ask, having completely lost track of the day, the time. It really doesn't seem to matter here.

Counting on his fingers, Juan concludes, 'It's Sunday.'

'Auntie Marg and I have a flight booked for tomorrow morning! Will we get back in time for that?' I ask, not wanting to tempt fate, but crossing all my fingers that this is a good sign. If Auntie Marg isn't OK to fly, I need to work out what I'm going to say to my family. If I get the chance, that is, assuming I don't get thrown in a Peruvian jail.

Juan nods. 'We have fuel, and the water is moving slowly so we should get back quickly.'

When our old boat got smashed to pieces, we had to snake our way to Juan's family home through narrow, shallow stretches of water, deep in the jungle. With this boat we can take a quicker, wider route back to

Iquitos, and a few hours after we leave Juan's family – we reach a town. I can see it ahead: white buildings gathered together on the edge of the water. A jetty, some boats, groups of people – and music. Drums and trumpets, I think?

'That is the only town, other than Iquitos, that I have ever been to,' Juan says proudly. 'Let's stop here!'

'Er, is that a good idea? Do we have time?' I ask. Part of me is relieved that we can delay what might turn out to be the worst day of my life if Auntie Marg is really badly hurt. The other part is worried that we don't have time for this!

But Juan is already pulling the little boat in the direction of the jetty. 'Yes! It will be worth it!' he says firmly.

He scans the shoreline for a mooring place, steering the boat expertly into a narrow gap between a large, grey, mean-looking boat and a small fishing boat with fancy yellow writing all over it. A friendly-looking man with massive arms and a red cap leans over the side of the fishing boat, nods and encourages us to tie our boat to his. His hand stretches over the side and he pulls me up and onto the deck of his boat effortlessly. Juan follows. '*Gracias*,' he says.

Juan and the man laugh as if they know each other. The man pats Juan on the arm, and with that Juan skips off the boat, down a walkway and onto the street. I have to run to catch up and as I leap onto the pavement, music, laughter and the distinctive smell of popcorn fill the air. The dusty pavement is warm underneath my bare feet.

'Welcome to carnival!' Juan shouts over his shoulder.

'What, like fête day? We have a carnival in our town and everyone dresses up. Is it like that?' I shout back over the drums and whistles.

I grab my phone as we walk into the main part of the town, switch it on and start snapping away. I'm holding it tighter than ever. It has valuable photos on it now, and I'm just hoping I have enough battery left for some more pictures!

Juan's leading us towards some music. I can't see where it's coming from, but I can hear it throbbing through the streets. Flashes of gold, pink and yellow appear; everyone is dressed in colourful clothes and costumes and there are people everywhere, drinking, laughing, smiling and dancing. They're actually dancing in the roads! It's the kind of dancing like they do on *Strictly*, up close and personal, only this is even more saucy. There are legs and arms flying about, and the women aren't wearing much more than underwear. Some look amazing. Some look a bit cringe; there's a dark-haired woman strutting her stuff up to a man wearing the tightest white trousers I have EVER seen. I click my camera as they spin into each other, chests bumping.

'I know this is a detour, but I knew you would like it,' Juan tells me, grinning.

'I do like it!' I call. I can't stop smiling or staring. After days in the jungle, it's so good to see buildings and people again.

Juan picks up the pace now, beginning to run, dodging around corners and weaving his way quickly down the street. He turns left into a dark side street; it's damp and smells funny and I'm not sure why he's brought me here, away from all the colour and music. Juan is shuffling sideways down the narrow alley, his back to the wall, peering through windows and doorways. He leans in through an open window and grabs something. His hands are suddenly full of sparkly colourful material and he's back in the alleyway and dashing past me. 'Come on!' he hisses.

'That's stealing!' I call after him, but Juan is already diving into another little side street.

'It is borrowing – we will give it back,' he reassures me. He's already shoving one arm through the sleeve of a bright blue jacket, with yellow and orange stitching. There are tassels down the arms and on the collar. He throws a bundle of blue and yellow cloth at me, and it's the weirdest thing I have ever put on; it's a shirt and a skirt combined, with feathers, buttons and tinsel-type material. Seriously, there's more on this top than we put on our Christmas tree. Juan is grinning and pointing and I try to pose but I can't stand up straight for laughing. As he adds a feather headdress, I take his photo and then pass him my phone so that he can take mine.

'You look ridiculous!' I tell him. With my phone battery flashing, I take a couple more quick photos – I really want to show these ones off, I mean *share* them, with Rebecca and Kate and Harpreet.

'So do you. Now we are ready for carnival!' declares Juan, adjusting the feathers on his headdress. He pulls my arm and drags me back into the busy street, dodging and darting in between people.

As we cross the street, side-stepping cars packed full of teenagers with music booming out of the windows, we head towards a mass of people. There are huge rows of metal seats, like the ones you see at a football stadium, only they all face towards the road and the glittery dancing people.

As we get nearer, we cross into what is obviously the car park, but it's jam-packed with people, not cars. We may look ridiculous in our borrowed outfits, but no one bats an eyelid, because in comparison Juan and I may as well be in a boring school uniform! Everyone is smiling, dancing, waving their arms in the air or shaking musical instruments, and their bodies are a mass of gold and glitter, feathers and flesh, teeth and tiaras. It's hard to tell where one person stops and another begins.

There are men on stilts, men carrying drums, men wearing huge headdresses ten times bigger than their heads. There are women wearing bikinis and feathers and not a lot else. All of them are dancing, and Juan is holding my hand tightly. Here it's a must – if I let go he'll be swallowed into the sea of swirling feathers and glitter in seconds.

En masse, shuffling and dancing, we move towards the stadium, the steel structure standing proud against the sky. It's an oblong building – a big running track with seats down both sides and a gap at each end. The crowd we're packed in with start proper dance routines as we head inside. Women in glittery high heels throw their legs onto each other's shoulders, swivelling their hips at lightning speed and spinning straight into the arms of the men, who wait for them with puffed-out chests and massive toothy grins.

I don't really know what's going on. All I can do is a cross between a step ball change I learned in a tap class Mam MADE me go to, and Gangnam style – but I love it. The crowds on both sides of the track are clapping and cheering. 'This is brilliant, Juan!' I scream over the top of the music.

Juan grins at me and points up to a group of glamorous men and women sitting in chairs on the tops of ladders, like umpires at a tennis match.

They're holding clipboards and watching the procession we're part of.

'The judges!' Juan shouts over the noise.

'Judges? What are they judging?'

In response, Juan nods enthusiastically and smiles. He can't have heard.

I grab my camera again and take another photo. I'm not sure I can do this amazing atmosphere justice! There's so much to look at – and the rhythm has got me.

Samba!

CHAPTER 27

Reluctantly, two coconut drinks and a questionable hot dog that Juan 'borrowed' later, we leave the glitter, the sparkle and the carnival behind. We run and put the costumes back where we found them, throwing the crumpled material through the open window.

The sun is setting but the streets are packed with even more people than before. Some carry huge crates of beer on their shoulders, some have babies strapped to their backs. The closer we get to the boats, tied up for days while their crew drink, dance and spin in a world of sequins, the quieter the music becomes.

We climb back onto the fishing boat next to ours and I am first to jump down into our own boat. Juan follows me a minute later, reaching into the back pocket of his shorts to show me something else he's 'borrowed'.

'That fisherman is nice. He will not mind,' he whispers, holding out two bananas and a bar of chocolate.

As we set off I break the chocolate into pieces and shove them in my mouth, practically inhaling them. I've missed chocolate.

Juan has already explained that if we set off tonight, sleep close to the riverbank and move again first thing, we'll be closing in on Iquitos early tomorrow morning. Because it's carnival, there aren't any other boats on the river around here – they're all parked up at that jetty. We're going upstream, against the flow of the water, but because there is no traffic we can move effortlessly to the slowest parts of the river and continue our journey quickly.

I shuffle my bum into the bottom of the boat, resting my head on the wooden side, watching the lily pads. This golden hour is my favourite part of every day here: the sun setting, the air warm, everything glowing.

A hollow thud, a tap, interrupts my thoughts and

I glance over the side of the boat, the early-evening sunshine bouncing off the water like a mirror. I squint to see what we hit, but there is nothing.

Then there's a loud breath as someone – something – exhales. There's a whiff of fish and that thud again. I shift to the other side of the boat and gesture to Juan to cut the engine.

Another breath, as if someone is blowing a raspberry, then, '*Look!*' I yell.

Behind Juan's head, a slice of pink breaks the surface of the water. Juan spins around, but it's already gone.

'*Look!*' I scream again as another flash of pink, more vivid than the first, appears to the right of our boat. It's only visible for a second before it disappears.

'Pink river dolphin!' says Juan, grinning.

I scan the surface of the water. A row of white teeth appear, a nose, then a tail, and I remember what the legend about pink dolphins involves: children being snatched and carried away, never to be seen again. But Juan doesn't look scared. Intrigued, excited, but not scared.

I slide my phone from its pouch and take a single

photo before turning it off and putting it on the floor of the boat. Then I shuffle to the side, swing my legs over, and slide into the water. I screw my eyes closed, hold my breath and dip beneath the surface for as long as I dare, waving my arms to keep me low enough so that Juan can't see me. I feel a gentle, playful nudge against my leg, then my arm. My lungs burning, I push back to the surface and grab the side of the boat, gasping for air and opening my eyes. There are three of them – three pink dolphins, splashing and diving around me.

I can see Juan's face peering over the side of the boat, mouth wide open, staring into the water.

'Come on in!' I call. 'Or are you scared they're going to kidnap you and turn you into a dolphin too?'

Juan grins and in a second dives into the water. The dolphins disappear, stunned by his sudden movement. As quickly as they disappeared, he reappears. His face is pained, panicked, and he's scrabbling to get straight back into the boat.

'What? What is it?' I call.

'Piranha!' Juan shouts, splashing about.

I grab the side of the boat and haul myself over. Juan's thrashing about and yelling, and I think he must actually have been hurt, because he doesn't seem to be able to climb back in. 'Here, I'll help you!' I shout. Quickly, I lean over the side, hook my arms underneath his armpits, then pull him into the boat. Our tangled bodies fall to the floor, the boat rocking underneath us.

The dolphins have disappeared, but in their place is a gang of small, silvery fish. I didn't think fish could look so mean, but one definitely has a spiky, spear-like tooth sticking out of its mouth.

Juan's leg is bleeding. I wipe away the blood pouring over his ankle to reveal an open, fleshy wound in his calf. He's breathing fast and his face is pale.

'Are you OK?' I ask.

'They are so fast!' he replies, swallowing hard and looking at his leg. 'They are attracted to blood . . . if more of the shoal had arrived before you pulled me into the boat . . .'

'Sit there,' I tell him firmly, taking charge. Then I rip a strip of material from the bottom of my borrowed T-shirt and help him to knot it tightly around his ankle. I've seen people do that in films. They make it look easier than it is, though.

'Thanks,' Juan tells me. He's smiling, and there's another, unfamiliar look on his face. He's impressed!

The bleeding has stopped and the colour is returning to his cheeks. Our journey upstream is still on track. I don't want to say anything, but I think I might have just done something right for once.

Trying hard not to smile too much, I take control of the boat. I steer us towards the riverbank on the far side, scanning for a place to park for the night.

'That will do.' Juan nods to a small inlet just off the main river. 'We'll get a few hours, then go again, and . . . thanks,' he repeats, patting his leg.

I nod. No need to say anything.

PINK RIVER DOLPHINS

Known as *el bufeo colorado*, these are only found in the Amazon. Legend suggests they can transform into men and walk onto dry land. Some people believe they snatch children and force them to live as dolphins. Others believe they fall in love with women they see on the shore.

Appearance:

Smaller than sea dolphins, with longer noses, river dolphins also have what look like fingers on the ends of their flippers. They get pinker when excited or surprised, like when a human blushes.

Top strength:

Very intelligent, their brains are typically 40% bigger than that of a human! Their long noses mean they can hunt and scavenge the bottom of the river bed and their eyesight is better than most sea dolphins.

Most likely to be found:

In fresh non-salty water. They are sociable and friendly. Have been seen in groups of 10-15, jumping over one another.

Deadly?

That depends on whether you believe the legend! If you are lucky enough to see a pink river dolphin, your heart will skip – but sadly they are under increasing threat. Environmental changes, dams and mining work mean they are struggling. Some get caught in boat propellers and there are even reports that some of the dolphins' fins are cut off by fishermen who then use them as bait, leaving the dolphin mutilated.

SCARE RATING: 42 • DANGER RATING: 60 • COOL RATING: 95

PIRANHA

There are about 20 species of piranha fish that live in the Amazon river and not all of them are aggressive – but those that are can be deadly! The most dangerous is the red-bellied piranha. They will eat almost anything alive, not even bothering to kill their prey before they begin to eat.

Appearance:

Usually about 14 to 26 cm long. They have a single row of sharp teeth in both their top and bottom jaws, and the teeth are tightly packed and interlocking. They tend to travel and attack in groups – or *shoals*.

Top strength:

Piranhas are famous for their deadly teeth, which are razor-sharp!

Most likely to be found:

They live in the Amazon basin and elsewhere in South America. They have also been found in China and Bangladesh.

Deadly?

Yes. Even baby piranhas are dangerous, and as soon as they reach about 4 cm long, they start eating the fins and flesh of other fish. A group of piranhas can strip an animal of all its flesh in a few minutes!

SCARE RATING: 85 • DANGER RATING: 90 • COOL RATING: 73

Dear Gav,

This might be my last ever email. If I am home
by the time you get this, just delete it. IF,
however, years have passed and you haven't
seen me, read on.

There is a small chance that I permanently
damaged Auntie Marg and got arrested and
put in a Peruvian jail, never to be seen again.
However, I wanted to let you know that all that
stuff we saw on the TV about pink dolphins
and caiman and scorpions – well, lots of it is
true. I even saw most of them myself! (Pictures
attached!)

I didn't get a photo with a caiman, but they
are bigger than I expected. Monkeys are the
best. Piranha are scary to look at, but if you
act fast around them and keep cool, you'll
be OK. There's no need to be scared of pink
river dolphins – they're not men trapped in the
bodies of dolphins out to steal children. I actually met some and yes, they kind of talk to each
other, but they didn't try to kidnap me or Juan.
They sort of played with me! I just wanted you
to know in case you ever get near one and you

don't know whether to be scared or excited.
You should be excited.

Basically, you can't believe everything you see
on TV – but you can learn some basic first aid,
so maybe in the future just pick your television
more carefully.

Love

Amy
x

CHAPTER 28

I don't think either of us slept much last night.

Juan and I talked a little bit about his family, how he misses his sister, but how he and Dudu would find it too painful to live with them all the time. I talked about my brother, and how writing him emails – even if I was just saving them in my drafts folder, and they weren't actually getting to him – stopped me getting homesick. Even though I officially hate him.

Mainly, though, we sat in silence, trying to pick animals out of the shadows. There were grunts from caiman and coos from the tree tops, but nothing scares me that much now. The only fear I have is that feeling, deep in my stomach, that Auntie Marg might not be OK. If it wasn't for that, I think I would be in my element here.

It's weird: the things I avoid doing at home – like brushing my teeth and having a shower – are now the things I crave. I want to wash my hair, feel clean. But I don't care about eating with a knife and fork, and I haven't missed TV or my iPad. I like falling asleep with the sounds of animals and birds around me. No two days are the same; if I don't see dolphins I see sloths, or birds, and sometimes all three.

My phone's finally run out of battery, so the sun has become my only clock, and as it begins to wake up, introducing the heat to the day, we untie our boat from its branch and set off again. We're down to our final few hours on the river.

'Juan, we're going to have to make a plan of action,' I say. What if Dudu's waiting for us on the shore as we pull in? 'If you can distract your dad when we get back, I'll go straight to the hospital to find Auntie Marg. Juan' – my voice is serious now – 'I promise I'll try and make good use of those pictures of the logging sites. Get something done, if I can. Auntie Marg knows loads of people who get stressed out about stuff like that, the environment and everything. She'll kick up a stink. And if she can't, I will,' I add, my eyes on the floor.

Within a couple of hours, our little engine still humming away, I spot Iquitos. The buildings, the boats, the houses. We have spent so many hours just looking at trees, it's hard not to get a little excited by the sight of our destination. As the buildings get bigger and we get nearer, I can make out the writing on signs, the open windows with lace curtains flapping in them, small groups of people drinking from brown bottles. I close my eyes and wish to every god I've ever heard of that Auntie Marg is OK.

I scan the shore, looking for Dudu, but there are so many boats and people swarming around there's no way of telling if he is there.

'Juan, listen. When we get back, I'm just going to run, head down, as fast as I can.' I know the sooner I get to the hospital, the sooner I can find out how she is.

The boat isn't even at a standstill when I leap onto the jetty, put my head down, throw one foot ahead of the other and plough my way through the bustling crowds. I daren't stop.

'Hang on a minute,' I mutter. 'I don't even know where the hospital is!'

My phone's dead so I can't look it up. What's the word in Spanish? 'Er . . . hospital? Hospital?' I ask a lady walking past me. She shoots me a funny look, but points down the next street – the Spanish for 'hospital' must be almost the same word! '*Gracias!*' I shout, running off.

I know I'm heading in the right direction when an ambulance drives past me. I reach a car park with a huge glass building ahead, and people moving in and out of wide glass doors.

I race in and up to reception. 'Margaret Wild?' I pant at the lady behind the desk.

She checks her computer, then points down a corridor and gestures for me to go up a flight of stairs. I follow her directions, peering through the doors on either side. Everything's shiny and clean-smelling. My heart's hammering in my chest.

Please let her be OK.

Please let her not be too angry with me.

Please let Dudu not be here.

I screech to a halt at a door with a thick glass

window in it, catching sight of her long red hair. She's sitting upright on a hospital bed, surrounded by suitcases and bags of photography kit, and wearing her normal clothes – well, not normal like a teacher would wear, but normal for Auntie Marg. Folds of long, floaty material, layers of bangles on one arm, and a cast on the other. She has a bruise on one cheek, and she looks slightly dazed, but when she sees me her face breaks into a huge smile.

'Amy, my darling! There you are!'

'You're OK!' I scream, running over and throwing my arms around her.

She winces and peels me off her. 'Of course I am! Just a few cuts and bruises, a fractured arm, two broken ribs and a sprained ankle – but nothing to worry about. It's so lovely to see you! I have to say, I've been very surprised that the hospital has been so strict about you visiting me. Only allowing Dudu to come! I've missed you. But I know he's been taking good care of you for me!'

I see a hint of confusion on her face as she clocks my bare feet and cropped hair. I don't know what to say. What is she talking about?

'I'm sorry you've been stuck watching videos with Juan all week,' she goes on. 'You must have been bored senseless. What are your parents going to say? I promised them I would get you doing something different, make you work hard and put your energy into something positive for once! Maybe we just won't tell them . . .' She winks at me.

I stare at her. This is music to my ears. 'Deal!' I confirm. But I still don't understand. Why isn't she angry with me?

'Dudu said you have behaved like an angel since my accident! I'm embarrassed to admit that I don't even remember what happened. I just know I was taking pictures on the river, I asked you for a different lens . . . and then my mind's blank! Dudu explained about those American tourists. So careless of them! I can't believe they ran me over!'

Someone clears their throat behind me, and I whirl round. 'Dudu!' I say, totally confused by the story Auntie Marg is telling me. It sounds like he has lied . . . for my benefit.

Dudu is staring at me like I'm a ghost. He nods

towards the corridor, stepping out of the room and out of earshot of Auntie Marg. I follow him.

'What's going on?' I ask nervously.

'I didn't know what I would do if you didn't come back today, Amy,' Dudu says quietly, shaking his head. He's *relieved*, I realize. 'Is Juan OK?' he asks, eyes wide, hands clasped.

'He's fine. Great. Just dandy,' I say. Oh no, this is it. He's getting ready for the interrogation, he's checking Juan is OK, then he's going to turn me over to the police.

'Don't you want to know why I covered for you?' Dudu asks.

I just look at him, waiting.

'I didn't want your aunt to think I am a monster. I didn't want to tell her you ran away because I was chasing you, because you were scared of me.' He sighs. 'I panicked when you disappeared. If anything happened to you, I knew she would blame me. She would hate me.'

'What?' I ask, confused. I hadn't thought about it like that. Dudu thought Auntie Marg would blame *him* for me disappearing?

'I searched every inch of Iquitos for you. When I saw Juan's boat had gone, I guessed you must have gone with him. I was worried. That jungle is dangerous. I have lost so much to it already. I can't go back there, but Juan insists on it. He feels he has to. I haven't slept for days, worried something would happen to both of you. I've been lying to your aunt, making up a story about some American tourists losing control of their tuk-tuk, praying you would both come back safely before she got out of here.'

'He's fine. We're both fine. Nothing dangerous happened,' I lie, trying to reassure him. 'We went to see your – his – the family.'

Dudu nods. 'Every time Juan goes, I think he won't come back. I know what he does there, and he'll get into serious trouble one day. I just worry because I love him. He's my only son. I remind him of the dangers, but he doesn't care.' Dudu shrugs.

'I think he does care,' I say. 'He cares a lot, about your family. Where you come from.' I probably shouldn't say anything, but I feel the need to defend Juan. Over the last few days, I've realized Juan isn't that weird. I really didn't expect Dudu to be like this.

Maybe it's not just my mam who worries – I think all parents do.

'So you're definitely not mad?' I check.

'You won't tell your aunt, will you?' He's almost begging me to go along with a lie that is, quite frankly, the best thing I have ever heard.

'Well . . . OK.' I bite the inside of my mouth to stop myself from laughing. This has worked out a million times better than I expected.

We smile at each other, and that's that. Our pact. Our fib to protect Auntie Marg, Dudu and me.

Inside the room, Auntie Marg is zipping up the last suitcase. 'Dudu, you're so very kind to have looked after Amy for me. But we really must go back to England, now that the doctors have said I am OK to fly,' she says. 'Amy, darling, our passports are on the side there. Look after them for me, would you? Dudu, as you know, is driving us straight from here to the airport. Apparently his tuk-tuk has a big dent in one side, but I've given him a special tip for taking such good care of you and he'll have it looking brand-new in no time. Now, let's go – we can't miss our flight. It seems months since we booked it! What a funny trip it's been. I'm so disappointed I couldn't take more pictures, but I hope I managed to get enough on that first day. Darling, I love your new hair! When did you get that done? Very pop star. Your clothes, too – those fabulous beads around your neck – how wonderful. Did you go shopping at the markets?'

CHAPTER 29

Throwing Auntie Marg's bags onto the battered tuk-tuk to join my own, which Dudu collected from the hotel days ago, I bundle Auntie Marg into the back seat. Her injuries make her movements awkward, but other than that, this is going well. The sooner we get on that plane and out of here, the less chance there is of Dudu mucking this up and telling her the truth.

As we set off, warm air and the occasional fly hit the back of my throat. Auntie Marg is firing questions at me about my 'quiet' week, and I nod and tell her what she wants to hear. She's still so confused – I could tell her anything and she'd believe me.

It feels like we're at the airport in minutes. As I start to pull our bags off the tuk-tuk, I can see Dudu gearing up to hug Auntie Marg. My opinion of him has totally changed. He's actually quite sweet, quite emotional. I grin at him – we'll both keep each other's secrets.

'Will you say goodbye to Juan for me?' I ask him. 'I left him in a bit of a hurry.'

Dudu nods. 'Of course.'

As we board the plane and take our seats, Auntie Marg wrinkles her nose and sniffs. 'Darling, when was the last time you had a wash? And we'd better get you some flip-flops at the next airport. You can't go home barefoot!' She shifts awkwardly in her rigid seat, trying to rest her injured arm comfortably, and I get a pang of guilt looking at her cast.

I'm going to make it up to you, Auntie Marg, I promise in my head. Even though you don't know there's anything to make up for. You can have first pick when we get a Chinese takeaway. You can always have the comfy chair when we watch a film, and I won't put bird food on top of your caravan ever again.

Auntie Marg gestures to the phone hanging around my neck. 'Come along then, darling, let me look at your pictures. Even though I didn't manage to take many myself, I want to see what you got!'

I rummage around in my bag and find the portable charger that Mam gave me, and plug the phone in. After a few seconds, the screen lights up. I open the photos folder and pass the phone across.

Auntie Marg starts to scroll through my photos, slowly at first, then more quickly. 'Amy, some of these are wonderful,' she gasps. 'Is that a view of Iquitos from . . . from a rooftop?'

'Oh, those?' I say, making a quick decision. 'They're the photos *you* took, Auntie Marg, and I helped you download them to a computer at the hotel and email them to me, so I had copies saved on my phone. Remember? It was just before the accident. It was so lucky we did it then, so almost everything was backed up digitally.' I know this technological language will baffle her – she won't question it.

'*I* took them?' Auntie Marg repeats, staring at the screen. 'Goodness – I really have forgotten so much of the past week. How hilarious. It's almost as if that little bump I had wiped my memory blank! What a shame I can't remember any of it. We managed to pack so much in, didn't we? Honestly, you were so clever to – what did you say? Back them up?'

'So . . . you think I was a good helper?' I ask.

'You were *wonderful*. Your parents are going to be so proud when I tell them how responsible and sensible you were, not making any fuss for Dudu while I was in hospital, and making sure all the photos I took were kept safe.' Auntie Marg waves the phone at me. 'This is looking a little bit worse for wear now, so we should really get you a new one when we get home.'

A wave of relief sweeps over my body. Auntie Marg is smiling and in one piece, I survived the jungle and made it back just in time for our flight home, *and* I might get a new phone.

Settling into my seat and waiting for the free pretzels, I catch a movement from outside. Dudu is waiting on the tarmac, ready to wave us off – and Juan has joined him! He's tanned and lean from our days on the river, and is smiling up at me.

I grin back – and then, without thinking, I press my hand to my lips and blow him a kiss. *What?!* Why did I do that! I can't believe I did that! I duck below the window. I can't look out again. I'm so embarrassed. I'm such an idiot!

Auntie Marg is still flicking through the camera, her expression curious at first, and then her mouth drops open. I've seen this before – she's excited. 'I can't believe it,' she breathes. 'These are brilliant! Are they . . . are they pink river dolphins? Amy, we've caught it all! How is this even possible? I can't even remember taking these! There's everything: beautiful children, wildlife . . . and is that . . . a logging site? Oh my goodness! Few people get so close to these sites. They're so dangerous and protected. The exposure, the storytelling – this is my best work ever!' She shoves the phone in front of my face. 'Look, darling! They've come out better than I could have dreamed! The magazine will *love* these. That means my book deal will happen too! Oh, Amy, it's so exciting.'

I look through the pictures. I remember the faces, the smiles, the crowded boats, the beady eyes of the crazy creatures. I remember it all: the sun on the river, the moon breaking through the trees . . . then a couple of Juan, looking moody generally, and then one where I've managed to catch him smiling.

'What do you think, Amy? Is this my best work yet? Don't you agree these are the best I've ever taken? *We've* taken. All those years of rubbish photos, wasted trips and rejections – but now I've done it, haven't I?' She frowns. 'I'll need to write up some notes, though. I wish I could remember where those pictures of the logging sites were taken – those images look quite shocking!'

'Oh, don't worry, Auntie Marg,' I say brightly. 'You made me take notes as you took the pictures, so I know *exactly* what the story about those loggers is. It's a good story to tell.'

She beams back at me. 'Well, that's perfect, Amy!' she cries. 'I've got some war wounds from this trip, but I don't care. It's worth it. I'll bring you again, my hard-working little good-luck charm!' She plants a kiss on my cheek and sits back happily in her seat, a smile of relief and satisfaction on her face.

I grin. 'Yes, Auntie Marg, it's worth it,' I tell her. 'Your best work yet.'

She can keep the photos. I don't mind.

After all, I have the spider.

AMY'S SPANISH DICTIONARY

Agua	Water
¡Allí está!	There she is!
Atención	Watch out
¡Ayúdenla!	Help her
Llorona	Crybaby
Bienvenido a . . .	Welcome to . . .
Bienvenido a casa	Welcome home
Buenas noches	Good night
Ella es un desastre	She's a disaster
A ella le estaba dando	
un ataque	She's having a tantrum
Ya es la hora	It's time
Al colegio	School
Otra vez usted está aquí	You're here again
Qué chica más tonta	You stupid irresponsible
e irresponsable	girl

Gracias	Thank you
Ha vuelto!	He's come back!
Hola	Hello
Lo antes posible	As soon as possible
Chica loca	Crazy girl
Lo siento	I'm sorry
Madre	Mother
Mañana por la noche?	Tomorrow evening?
Ve a buscar a alguien que nos ayude	Get help
Permíteme	Allow me
Pescado	Fish (when ready to eat)
Por aquí	Over here
Por favor	Please
Quédense aquí	Stay there
Quién?	Who's this?
Relájese	Relax
Río	River
A dormir	Bedtime
Le duele?	Does it hurt?
Tía	Aunt
Usted pudo haberla matado!	You could have killed her!

Mire el daño!	Look at the damage!
Vámonos	Let's go